Pendulum
Book One of the Nora Pepper Paranormal Series
ROBIN A. DEVEREAUX

Copyright © 2015 by Robin A. Devereaux-Nelson

All rights reserved. No part of this publication may be reproduced, distributed, or transmitted in any form or by any means, including photocopying, recording, or other electronic or mechanical methods, without the prior written permission of the publisher, except in the case of brief quotations embodied in critical reviews and certain other noncommercial uses permitted by copyright law. For permission requests, please email the publisher, addressed "Attention: Permissions Coordinator," at the address below.

This is a work of fiction. Names, characters, businesses, places, events and incidents are either the products of the author's imagination or used in a fictitious manner. Any resemblance to actual persons, living or dead, or actual events is purely coincidental.

FarmGirl Publishing
Saginaw and Bay City, MI
robindevereaux@gmail.com

For Emily

Constant reader and gift sister

1

All the fish were belly up in the pond. Nora Pepper stood at the window looking out at the wide expanse of lawn, brilliantly manicured and landscaped. Behind the closed door of the service bathroom off the professionally appointed kitchen Nora could hear Vivian Waldemar-Spruce retching. Nora tried to ignore the sound and her own rising gorge. Gag reflex. Instead, she stared at the pond and the bright orange and white abstract designs of the expensive Megalotis fish lying on their sides winking in the sun like jewels. Other than the floating bodies, the garden and pond were perfection. No doubt the grounds had been recently maintained and some extra floral arrangements seemed to have been planted as well, Nora guessed, for the elder Waldemar's anniversary party which she'd been hired to cater. Seeing the expensive fish floating on the pond made Nora doubt her decision once again to contract with Vivian – even though the woman had once been her closest friend. While it was probably some sort of gardening error – a wrongly used additive or pesticide – Nora couldn't help feeling a cold chill every time she found herself glancing out at the ruined pond.

Behind her the bathroom door opened, and Nora turned to see Vivian emerge, her face white and drawn. She'd pulled her long, blonde hair back into a pony-tail, a style she probably hadn't sported since she'd attended Clarence Ridgemont High School where she and Nora met fifteen years earlier. Vivian went into the butler's pantry and came out holding a bottle of Stolichnaya. Nora raised an eyebrow as she watched her former friend drop two ice cubes into a glass and add a healthy shot of the vodka.

"What?" Vivian said, meeting Nora's eyes after taking a drink of the liquor. "Judging me? Again?"

Nora turned back to the window and sighed. She pushed a strand of her long, unruly dark hair behind her ear. "No," she said, but in her head she thought she was judging. A little anyhow. After all, it was only nine fifteen in the morning. A little early for vodka, even if you were Vivian Waldemar-Spruce, who was probably the wealthiest woman in Ashton Bay, other than her grandmother, Doris Waldemar, that is. Nora listened to the sound of Vivian drinking, then ice cubes knocking back into the empty glass.

"We used to be friends," Vivian said softly as she set her glass in the stainless steel sink.

"Yes," Nora said. "We did."

"That was a long time ago."

"I suppose." Nora watched as a man in overalls approached the edge of the pond. He put his hands on his hips and shook his head, then walked back toward a large, white panel truck parked near the edge of the gardens.

Vivian joined Nora at the window. She shuddered a little as she looked out. "I'm - frightened," she said.

Nora turned to her. "Why?" she asked. She studied Vivian's face, watched her chin quiver. Vivian cocked a shoulder noncommittally. It was a tell Nora knew well. It was stubborn Vivian not wanting to say anything. "Do you think someone did this? On purpose, maybe?"

Vivian opened her mouth to speak, then clamped it closed again. She shifted her eyes away from Nora's. "I – I don't know," she stammered. "I mean, there've been some things – happening. On the property."

Nora sensed the other woman's anxiety vibrating in her own stomach. Felt Vivian's fear. She got that feeling suddenly, that drifting feeling she hated. She took a deep breath and blinked hard, shutting the unwanted sensation down. "What kinds of things?" Nora asked. "You know, if someone has been giving you and Daniel trouble I could call Lucien for you -."

"No," Vivian interrupted, her demeanor suddenly changing. "No police. It's not that kind of thing-." She stopped herself, shook her head then reached back and pulled the band from her hair, her blonde locks flowing over her shoulders like golden water. "That's not necessary." Her mouth turned hard, her eyes colder. "I've had a new maintenance company in. For the party. One of the crew must have used some sort of chemical or pesticide or something they shouldn't have. That's all. I'm sure it's nothing – like that. Nothing – criminal."

For a moment the two women eyed one another. The sight of Vivian's white face tugged at Nora, even though she tried to push the feeling down. It was plain that her former friend was stressed out, scared even. Nora cleared her throat. "Vivian," she said, reaching out toward her. "If – if I can help-"

Vivian took a step back and straightened her cardigan sweater. She touched the gold necklace at her throat. "I'll leave you to your work," Vivian said, turning and heading for the kitchen door.

Nora frowned. Frightened one moment, ice queen the next? "Vivian?" she called.

The other woman stopped and turned, her face a mask. "Yes?"

Nora felt the drifting feeling again and saw out of her peripheral vision a shadow pass near the other woman who trembled slightly as it washed over her. Nora blinked, gooseflesh rising on her arms. "Nothing," she said, wanting it to be so. "It's nothing."

2

Nora liked working alone. Even though she was cooking for a larger party on her own – twenty-five people – she knew that she'd planned carefully and everything would be completed in time. When Kat arrived with the servers they'd hired, she could brief them on the meal and then she get the heck out of there, leaving Kat in charge before she'd be forced to run into the particularly handsome Daniel Spruce. She knew it was silly – their brief relationship had happened years ago. However, the pain of youth still stung to some degree and that embarrassed Nora. More than anything she disliked embarrassment and awkward encounters, and she was afraid that was exactly what would happen if forced into a conversation with Daniel. Best to let *that* sleeping dog lie, she thought. She stepped up the pace on the cleaning and de-veining of the prawns she was preparing for the appetizer.

As she ran cold water over the large shrimp, she chided herself for how quickly she'd offered to get in touch with Lucien on Vivian's behalf. There was one dog she had trouble letting lie, no matter how hard she tried. Though divorced for nearly two years now, she and Lucien had stayed on fairly good terms – which at once Nora thought was a good and a not-so-good thing. The divorce had been bittersweet, neither doubting that they loved one another, but that love was not enough to mend the rift between them that his demanding job as a detective and her own personal struggles created between them. After three years of marriage, they'd called it quits, used a mutual lawyer and left the marriage with what each of them had come in with. They'd sold their house, splitting the profit, which Nora used to start Pepper Pot, the personal chef and catering business she owned, managed with the help of her closest friend, Kat Kalinowski.

She and Lucien still managed to run into one another often, whether by design or chance. In fact, she'd bumped into him just that morning, when she'd gone to pick up the seafood and fish she'd ordered for Vivian's party. When she'd told him she was doing a job for Vivian Spruce, he'd rolled his eyes and had gotten that maddening half smile on his face she hated and found adorable at the same time. She supposed running into him as often as she did wasn't surprising in a small town like Ashton Bay, but in her gut Nora knew their meetings weren't always completely serendipitous, but by Lucien's design and hers, if she was honest with herself. After all, there were people she knew who lived in Ashton Bay who she didn't run into for years at a time – like Vivian Waldemar-Spruce, whom she'd been very successful at avoiding for at least five years, and maybe more, before bumping into her by chance at Keene's Flowers downtown.

It was Vivian's voice Nora had recognized first. Throaty and melodic. She'd met Vivian in choir class when they were freshmen at Clarence Ridgemont High School. Both altos, they'd ended up standing side by side in class. Somehow, against the odds, they'd become the best of friends, rich and beautiful Vivian and Nora, the child of working-class family with a rumor-riddled past. Nora suspected Vivian's friendship with her was partly an act of rebellion against the wealthy grandparents who were Vivian's guardians, but she'd pushed that aside, ignoring her own mother's remonstrations, until – well, until Daniel Spruce.

So, that day in the florists when Nora heard the all too familiar voice of Vivian planning the floral arrangements for her parents' anniversary party, her first instinct had been to bolt from the shop. She'd only needed a few greens for a dinner party she was catering, and on second thought suddenly felt she could do without them. She turned and put her hand on the door, but behind her Vivian had turned as well.

"Nora? Nora Pepper?" Vivian arched an eyebrow and one of her show-stopping smiles lit up her face.

"Vivian," Nora said, forcing a half-smile. She took a hesitant step toward the other woman, feeling a bit like a trapped rat.

"I've been meaning to call you for days," Vivian said. "How odd to run into you."

"Yes, well, you know I'm awfully-" Nora shot a hopeful glance toward the door.

"I need you," Vivian said. "I've had to fire the caterer I'd hired – and my grandparent's anniversary party is next weekend. Could you do it? I've heard positively wonderful things about you. I pay...very well."

"Listen, Vivian, I'm sure that's true, but I –"

Vivian wrinkled her nose in a way most people thought was charming, but in that moment irritated Nora. "You're not still upset about all that old high school stuff, are you?"

Nora's face colored. "I – of course not," she said quickly.

"Well, then," Vivian began, taking Nora's arm and pulling her toward the counter. "Let me tell you what I have in mind, shall we?"

Now here Nora was, working for the woman who'd betrayed her as a girl. She sighed and added her special blend of spices and a cut lemon to the pot of boiling water and plunged the basket of cleaned shrimp into the water. She watched them carefully, not wanting to overcook them, then pulled the shrimp from the pot and set them in the ice bath she'd prepared. She'd clean the branzino next, beautiful, whole fish she'd found at the fresh market just that morning. Thinking about the fish brought her around once again to Lucien. What the hell had he been doing at the fish market, of all places? And at six a.m. to boot. Had he been looking for her? She sighed. Enough of that, she said to herself, pushing his dusky, handsome face out of her mind. She shook her head, one of her long, dark curls escaping from her scarf and tickling her face, and turned back to the branzino. She was planning to roast them whole with lemon and purple potatoes, and then serve them on the long rectangle platter Bernie had made at her pottery studio. She thought about how lovely the white fish, bright green herbs and purple potatoes would look lying against the seafoam glaze on the platter. She smiled thinking about her grandmother, and how Bernie Pepper would cringe at the thought of the Waldemars eating from one of her gorgeous ceramic pieces. Bernie was not impressed by money or status or the Waldemar family, and she wasn't shy about saying it, either.

  Nora scooped the cooked shrimp out of the ice bath with her hands and placed them in a colander to drain, then turned to the fish lying on a bed of ice in a large, flat pan. She was particularly pleased with them. They were plump and their silvery skins looked like platinum, their eyes unclouded. They were very fresh. She'd had the fish man flay them open, remove the organs and wash them to save her some time in the kitchen. The meat inside was white and delicate. Nora planned to make diagonal slits on the skin of each fish and lay lemon slices and herbs inside and allow them to marinate until it was time to get them in the oven. She sharpened her knife, looking out the window at the perfect day.

  In the garden she could see Vivian standing with her arms crossed speaking to the man she'd seen earlier. He was wearing green work dungarees and a hat pulled low over his eyes obscuring his face. From the way he was looking at his shoes Nora surmised he was getting a good bawling out about the pond. As Vivian stalked away, Nora turned to reach for the first branzino. From the corner of her eye, she sensed a darkening in the garden and heard a sudden and tumultuous breeze kick up which disturbed the wind chimes that hung just outside the kitchen window. There was a slight, almost imperceptible movement near her, and as the kitchen darkened and the chimes jangled, she looked down to see the branzino she was reaching toward quickly snap it's jaw, it's tiny teeth clamping down on her finger, drawing blood. She cried out, pulling her hand back, her knife clattering to the floor. Outside the sound of the wind chimes tolled, filling the room with their maddening jangling. Nora's eye was drawn to the pond. There she saw two little girls standing at the water's edge, holding hands. They stood in the shallow water seemed to be staring directly in at Nora through the kitchen window. There was something disturbingly familiar about them, as if she'd seen them somewhere before.

  She took a step toward the window, clutching her wounded finger to her apron. The gardener was digging around in his cart for some tool or other, oblivious to the children. Then, just as suddenly as it had darkened, the sky cleared and Nora blinked as the twins disappeared along with the sudden darkness. Her heart thudded in her chest. She turned toward the counter where the branzino laid on their bed of ice, their gullets flayed open, dead, unmoving. Still her finger throbbed, and as she pulled her apron away from it, proof of the wound stained the white, cotton fabric. There were also two tiny puncture wounds on her skin that seemed to have stopped bleeding for the most part, but when she pressed on the pad of her finger, three fresh, bright red droplets appeared on her skin.

Nora's let out her breath and licked her lips to wet them. She opened the kitchen door and walked purposefully across the patio toward the gardener, who was pulling a large, green plastic pail out of his cart. As he set it down, he looked up at her and put his hands on his hips. "Ever see anything like this?" he said. "What a waste of money." In the pond the Megalotis floated like so many orange and white plastic pool toys.

"Where did those little girls go?" Nora demanded. Her voice trembled a little. She cleared her throat.

"What are you talkin' about, lady?" the gardener replied.

"The little girls," Nora said. "They were standing - right there." She pointed to the spot where the man had set the green bucket. Lying next to it was a long handled rake.

The gardener bent over and grasped the rake. He stood up and dragged its teeth across the surface of the pond, raking dead fish onto the pebbles that surrounded it. He shook his head at her, as if she were crazy. "I don't know what you're talkin' about," he said. "These people ain't got no kids." .

"No, I – I know that," Nora said. "But there were two little girls. Standing right here. You must have seen them."

"Lady," the gardener said gruffly. "There ain't no kids here."

Nora turned away, her stomach clenching. Behind her the gardener muttered to himself. She smoothed down her apron, the strawberry of blood still blooming bright red, damp and real on its surface. She swallowed. It was happening again, she thought miserably. It was happening again and she would do whatever she had to do to stop it.

3

It had been little things when she was a kid, odd things, and rarely scary. Things like knowing which book her teacher was going to read for story time, or what was in a brightly wrapped Christmas box. Sometimes she would have dreams about things before they happened. Like the time Nora's mother, Ivy, accidentally lost her wedding ring in the Thanksgiving turkey. Ivy hadn't noticed it was missing until all the guests had arrived and she was in the upstairs bathroom putting the finishing touches on her hair. As she sprayed the gaseous-smelling AquaNet on her carefully curled and backcombed locks, six-year-old Nora sat on the edge of the bathtub watching her mother primp. Ivy always got a little anxious when the family got together, and she wasn't particularly fond of her husband's mother and aunts, but Nora loved having the house full of people.

Ivy set the hairspray can on the edge of the sink and peered at her hand. "Nora, run down to the kitchen and get Momma's ring out of the little dish by the sink."

Nora sat on the porcelain tub edge, swinging one foot. "It's not in the dish, Momma," she said.

Ivy turned impatiently. "Do what I'm asking you, young lady," she said, one eyebrow raising in that way Nora didn't like. She sighed and got up and walked toward the door resolutely. She knew the ring wasn't there. It was inside the turkey that was filling the house with the fragrance of sage and oranges.

"Okay," she pouted, then under her breath. "But it's not there."

Ivy's quick hand reached out and grasped Nora hard on the arm. The little girl stopped short as Ivy leaned down and grasped her face in one hand. "I do not need you being sassy today," she said, her cigarette breath wafting over Nora's face. "Do you understand?"

Nora hung her head. "Yes, Momma," she said, turning on her heel, tears forming in her eyes.

She returned a few moments later with the empty ring dish and handed it to her mother. "Shit!" Ivy exclaimed, then set the dish down hard on the vanity. She gave herself a last look in the mirror. Downstairs, Gramma Bernie's loud laugh could be heard, and Ivy scowled. She gave Nora a sidelong look. "Go brush your hair," she said. "Then go downstairs with your cousins."

"It's in the turkey, Momma," Nora said.

Ivy sighed impatiently. "What's in the turkey?"

"Your ring," Nora said. "It is, Momma."

"Really. And just how do you know that, miss? Since you and your father slept until I had everything in the oven?"

"I – I - dreamed it, Momma," Nora said, swallowing hard. She knew what was coming, but the thought of being right over her mother's objections glittered in her mind like a shiny ornament.

Ivy's mouth formed a hard line. "I've told you more than once I don't want to hear any of that - talk. Do you hear me?" Ivy handed Nora the hair brush. "Now, brush that mop and get your fanny downstairs. And keep your little mouth shut." She turned and wiped at a smudge of lipstick at the corner of her mouth. "That's all I need is you starting up more craziness with Bernie and Bobbi," she muttered to herself.

"Yes, Momma," Nora said resolutely as her mother left the bathroom swirling with the aroma of Chanel Number Five.

Later, at the dinner table in a bustle of conversation and the clinking of silverware on the good china, Ivy lifted a forkful of her chestnut stuffing to her mouth and bit down on the gold band. She spit it out into her palm, her glance shooting across the table at Nora.

"What is it?" Charlie Pepper asked his wife.

Ivy stared daggers into Nora. "Did you put that in there?" she asked.

Coldness crept into Nora's stomach as the chatter at the table got quiet and everyone looked at her. "No, Momma," she whispered, "I told you, I-"

"You took my ring out of the dish and put it in there, didn't you!" Ivy accused.

Tears welled in Nora's eyes and her face flushed red as everyone at the table turned and stared at her. "Momma, I swear —" she began.

"That's enough!" Ivy said. "Go to your room!"

"What's going on?" Gramma Bernie asked.

"Never mind, Bernie." Ivy's voice was icy. "Nora, I said go to your room."

"But, Momma-" Nora began, her lip trembling.

"Ivy –" Charlie Pepper said. "It's Thanksgiving...: His wife threw him a withering glance. Charlie's face colored the same shade as Nora's and he lifted his wine glass and took a drink. Bernie glowered at Ivy across the table. One of the cousins snickered.

"Go," Ivy said, focusing her sharp eyes on her daughter. Nora knew from the tone of her mother's voice it was best not to argue. She got up from the table, her face burning with shame. She could feel the eyes on her back and hear her cousins whispering as she exited the dining room and began to climb the stairs.

Much later, Nora woke to someone softly stroking her back. She turned over and blinked to see Gramma Bernie sitting on the edge of the bed. "Hey, Bunny," her grandmother said, smiling.

Nora liked it when Gramma Bernie called her that. It made her feel small and soft and cuddly like a baby rabbit. "Hi, Gramma," Nora said, rolling over. She laid her head on her grandmother's thigh and the older woman continued rubbing Nora's back. It felt so good and Nora closed her eyes again, and breathed in her grandmother's woody scent. She liked that, too, that smell. Gramma Bernie always smelled like the piney woods that surrounded her little cottage out on River Road. That smell always made Nora feel safe, calm.

"You knew where your momma's ring was, didn't you, Bunny?"

Nora opened her eyes and nodded. It felt different when Gramma Bernie asked her about it. Not like she was going to get in trouble.

"How did you know?" her grandmother asked.

"I dreamed it," Nora said. "Last night."

Grandma Bernie's hand continued to stroke Nora's back soothingly. "Tell me about it," she said gently.

So, Nora told her about the dream. In it a big, fat turkey was walking around in their house. He was funny, walking around with a big cigar in his mouth. He was wearing a top hat and shiny, black shoes. He'd gone straight into the kitchen, his shoes tap-tapping on the waxed linoleum floor, stopping at the double sink where her momma's ring laid in the little, blue glass dish. Momma always put it there when she was cooking or washing dishes. The turkey had winked at Nora conspiratorially then plucked the ring from the dish, removed the cigar from his mouth with a flourish, blowing out an unreasonably large cloud of smoke in the process. Then he proceeded to swallow the gold ring. Nora watched his throat swell as it went down, like in the cartoons. He then patted his belly with a fat wing and strode out of the house.

Grandma Bernie chuckled. "That was a funny dream, wasn't it?" she said, grinning. Nora felt a smile creeping onto her own face. It felt good to smile. She nodded. "That's not the first time you had a dream like that, is it, Bunny? A dream that ended up happening? Not happening exactly like the dream but – you know what I mean, don't you, honey?"

Nora nodded her head.

"Hmmmm," Gramma Bernie said. "I thought so." She patted Nora's shoulder. "Listen, Bunny." Nora's grandmother lay down on the narrow bed and cuddled her granddaughter in her arms. "I know your mom gets nervous about – dreams like that. I also know it's good to talk to someone about them. So, you can always talk to me about it, okay? Or Auntie Bobbi." Bobbi was Gramma Bernie's older sister. Nora's mom said she was nutty as a fruitcake.

Nora nodded. She snuggled in her grandmother's arms. Daddy must have gotten his snuggliness from Gramma, she thought. He snuggled exactly like Gramma Bernie. "When you're older," Gramma Bernie whispered in her hair. "I'll explain everything. Okay?"

Nora's eyes fluttered. "Uh-huh," she said, yawning. She didn't want to think about dreams of turkeys, or Momma's glare or her snickering, snotty cousins. She just wanted to lie here in her grandmother's arms and go back to sleep. So, that was exactly what she did.

4

It was slightly less than an hour before dinner was served. Guests had arrived and were in the salon having drinks. Nora was cutting garnishes, scowling. One of the servers hadn't shown up, and the one that Kat had gotten on the fly, Jessie, was so new Nora didn't feel comfortable leaving her friend on her own with her. She finished the garnishes and rinsed her hands in the sink.

"Hey, Kat," she said as the other woman reached for the tray of garnishes. "I'm going to stay and help serve."

Kat threw a glance at the new girl, who was primping on the other side of the kitchen. She grinned at Nora. "What?" she said. "Too pretty?" It was their code for a server who had good looks but little common sense.

"You know her better than I do," Nora said, "But-".

Kat patted Nora on the arm. "Look," she said. "It's the Waldemars. It's a big deal. I'd appreciate it if you'd help serve. Anyway, you know how these folks are. They like having the chef 'explain the menu'." Kat laughed.

"You do that just as well, if not better than I do, and you know it."

Kat winked. "I do know it," she said, heading toward the new girl with the tray.

"Don't let her mess up the garnishes," Nora hissed.

"As if," Kat replied.

Nora headed in to the service bathroom. She stood before the mirror bathroom and buttoned the clean, black chef's coat over the white men's tee shirt she favored when she was cooking. It would have to do, though she was a stickler for her servers wearing pristine, white tuxedo shirts and black pants or skirts. In her experience, however, Kat was right - customers liked seeing her in the chef's coat. They like hearing her tell them about the food, the herbs and spices, roasting and grilling and folding. It made them feel like they were getting more for their money. A real professional.

She sighed. Her hair was a ruin. She'd had it tucked up in one of her exotic, colored scarves all day and she felt sweaty and disheveled. She winced, thinking about having to face Daniel Spruce looking like a rung out rag. She pulled her long, curly, dark hair back and secured it with a couple of bobby pins. She would have to don a clean scarf, she thought. She was pretty sure she had one and a pair of silver hoop earrings in the Jeep console as well. With those and a spot of lipstick, she thought she'd be passable – enough anyway, to help serve at the party. Mostly, she wanted to blend in with her staff. She hoped none of Vivian's guests expected her to entertain them for long. Nora didn't especially like schmoozing, but she did it when she had to. Business was business.

In the kitchen, Nora carefully whisked the lemon-basil vinaigrette she'd made earlier and tossed it into the salad. Kat helped her place the mixture of greens and herbs in the expensive wooden salad bowls Vivian had provided, and then they loaded them on large silver trays. Kat and Jessie hoisted them on their shoulders and headed toward the dining room, where the murmuring and laughter of the guests could be heard. Nora turned toward the oven to check the fish, and as she did, a movement outside the kitchen window caught the corner of her eye. As she looked up toward it, the wind chimes outside the window began to tinkle softly. There, standing at the edge of the koi pond once again, were the two little girls, holding hands.

<u>5</u>

Bernie Pepper wiped her hands on her flowered apron, streaks of melted chocolate smearing over her flat belly. Next to her, Bobbi reached out, her chubby, palsied fingers trembling a little, toward the warm shortbread. Bernie gave her a gentle swat on the hand. "Good grief, Roberta, can't you wait?" she said to her sister.

"Not when you're as old as I am, you can't," Bobbi replied, pursing her lips. "Every second counts."

"Oh, go on then," Bernie said. "But the chocolate's hot. So, be careful." She watched Bobbi bite into the gooey cookie, and a smile spread across her older sister's lips. "Good?"

"Marvelous," Bobbi purred. She placed her half-cookie on the edge of her tea saucer, picked up her cup and drank. "I swear, sister, you could make just as money if not more on your baked goods than you do on your pots." Bernie saw Bobbi's hand tremble slightly, which made her heart sore. In her day, her older sister had been so willowy and graceful. Bernie did her the kindness of trying her best not to notice Bobbi's infirmity, but as they both got older doing so was getting harder and harder.

Bernie turned and continued plating the warm shortbread. She could feel Bobbi's gaze on her. It made the skin on her cheek hot.

"When are we going to talk about it?" Bobbi said, finally.

Bernie sighed. Of course she knew exactly what her sister was talking about. "What good will it do?" Bernie answered sourly.

"Well, she's going to have to face it sooner or later, isn't she?" Bobbi said, just as sourly.

Bernie turned to her sister, exasperated. "Why must we always converse in questions?"

"Were we conversing," Bobbi said, popping the last bite of her shortbread into her grinning mouth. "I thought we were starting an argument."

Bernie pulled a chair out and sat down at the old wooden table across from her sister. She patted Bobbi's hand. "I don't want to argue with you, sister," she said.

"Nor I you."

"We both want the same thing," they said at the very same time, then smiled at one another, chuckling. They often did things like that. They were Pepper women, after all. It was part of who they were. Now, what they wanted – what they'd always wanted – was for Bernie's granddaughter, Nora, to accept herself as one of them. To honor her gifts. But like all Pepper women, she was a damn stubborn cuss. And as for Nora, she was especially so, having her mother's genes added to the mix. Everyone knew that Ivy Barrette was a hard woman. How in the world her gentle Charlie had ever married her was a mystery that had never revealed itself to the normally astute Bernie Pepper, much to her chagrin.

Bernie picked up a piece of shortbread from the platter and bit into it. It was good, warm and sweet and buttery. Next to creating the expensive ceramic platters and bowls she was known for in Ashton Bay and far beyond, she thought she probably liked baking best. Kneading and shaping dough or clay grounded her, made her feel the blood of ancient women – her ancestors - rise in her. Creating made her feel alive, and she'd needed that, especially since losing Chase Delacoix, the man she'd believed to be the love of her life. But it was losing their son, Charlie, Nora's father that had been the real love of her life. Her shining star. Now that he was gone as well, it was Nora she loved most fiercely. Nora, in whose eyes and smile she could see reminders of her beloved Charlie and Chase. All she wanted was Nora's happiness, and that wasn't going to happen for her granddaughter until she gave in and faced who – and what - she truly was.

The two elderly women sat together in comfortable silence sipping their tea. Bernie and Bobbi were two peas in a pod and neither of them craved nor gave into idle chatting. Outside the old log home they shared a sudden breeze came up, causing the branches of the old maple outside the window to brush its long, graceful branches against the metal roof. They looked at one another, and Bernie nodded. She'll need us, they both thought at once. Soon. Soon.

6

The courses were taking longer than Nora would have liked, and by the time Vivian was ready for the staff to serve the main course, Nora was already feeling edgy and on the verge of crankiness. She'd started feeling that was after seeing the twin girls standing at the edge of the pond for the second time that day. She still couldn't shake the feeling that she had seen them somewhere before. Added to that, the new girl had proved not only to have more good looks than common sense, but to be butter-fingered as well. She'd dropped an entire bowl of perfectly cut lemon peel roses scattering them across the kitchen floor, and elbowed the large bowl of prepared salad which an adept Kat had barely rescued by clutching it to her middle like she'd just received a forward pass. After the salad incident, Kat had given the girl a clean, white apron and kept her in the kitchen washing dishes, ignoring the young woman's tears and apologies. Better safe than sorry.

Nora and Kat put the finishing touches on the platter of baked branzino. Bernie's platter was glazed in a marvelous shade of aquamarine, imitating the sea. It was nearly three feet long, and despite the thinness of the ceramic, quite heavy. It had been one of her prize pieces, designed especially for her granddaughter, and Nora was happy to have an occasion to show it off. Nora and Kat had placed it on a wheeled cart draped in pristine, white linen. Nora's artistic arrangement of greens, florals and herbs were the perfect backdrop to display the delicate, fragrant fish, and when they wheeled it into the room, conversation stopped and sighs of *ooooooh* and *ahhhhh* took its place. Nora noted Vivian's look of satisfaction at her guests' response, and from across the room she caught Nora's eye and nodded.

Kat wheeled the cart to the waiting banquette and together she and Nora lifted the platter, tilting it slightly toward their hostess for her approval. Vivian smiled and stood, then she picked up her knife and clinked it on her water glass, and the entire table erupted in clapping. "Bravo, Nora!" Vivian said. "That looks splendid!" Nora's face colored. She looked sidelong at Kat who gave her a knowing look. Nora's love was being in the kitchen creating and she disliked this kind of attention, however she gracefully tipped her head at Vivian, and then she and Kat placed the platter carefully on the banquette. Kat raised a hand gesturing to the servers to begin, and they stepped forward and started serving the party guests. Nora stood to the side, looking a last time at the perfect platter of fish and as she did, she felt a stinging in her fingers. Looking down, she saw that blood had bloomed once again beneath the bandages where she'd been bitten. Just then, the lights in the dining room flickered, and Nora suddenly felt a swoopy, sick feeling in her belly. Everyone looked up at the flickering lights.

Just then, a sound began, barely noticeable at first, rhythmic and hollow, like the beat of a small drum or a clock. Nora looked around and could see the looks on the faces of the party guests. It was apparent they were hearing it, too. Vivian turned impatiently toward Daniel. "What is that?" she demanded.

"I have no idea," he replied.

"Well, do – something!" she shouted, and Daniel's face flushed. He stood there helplessly, his hands at his sides.

The sound grew louder, and the lights continued to flicker. Nora was suddenly cold. The sick feeling in her stomach increased. Kat stepped forward. "Perhaps it's something to do with the water system," she said, always reasonable. "Mr. Spruce, why don't we check the basement?"

Daniel threw Kat a relieved look. "Yes, of course," she said and followed her out of the dining room.

At the table, Doris Waldemar, Vivian's grandmother, leaned toward her husband, Glenn. The man had gone completely white and was staring, wide-eyed toward the grand staircase that lay in the hall just outside the dining room. He clutched suddenly at his chest, a pained look in his eyes. Nora followed his gaze, and there, at the base of the stairs near an immense, mahogany grandfather clock stood the two little girls, holding hands. The ticking grew louder, and louder, the large, brass pendulum of the clock swinging back and forth. The sound grew so loud that several of the guests were clutching at their ears. The flickering of the lights became more rampant, and beneath Nora's feet the floor seemed to sway and bend and then suddenly, there was a crashing sound. Nora looked up to see the grandfather clock falling forward, its glass doors shattering. All the lights in the house went out and everything was black.

In the darkness, Nora could barely breathe. Then, on either side of her were the twin girls. They each took one of her hands, and the coldness of their touch crept up Nora's arms and into her belly.

"*It's time*," said one.

"*There are no secrets that time does not reveal*," said the other.

Then the coldness in Nora's stomach was replaced by blackness swirling around her and she was falling into the abyss.

7

Lily and Lucy floated, hand in hand. Above their heads a million stars whispered and winked. Lily was humming. It was the song Daddy used to sing to them when he would sneak into the nursery late at night, his breath smelling sweet and pungent. "Every time it rains, it rains pennies from heaven..." The humming was annoying Lucy. She didn't want to think about Daddy. She just wanted to float and stare at the stars and contemplate what they would do next. "Stop it," she thought and squeezed her sister's hand. "Don't you know each cloud contains pennies from heaven," she heard Lily thinking back. Then, "No, I don't want to. I like that song." Lucy squeezed harder but got no response from Lily. She didn't know what she was expecting. The sisters were far beyond being able to feel any kind of pain, but Lucy knew very well how to get Lily's attention. She let go of her sister's hand.

The humming stopped abruptly.

Lily's hand snaked through the water like a lightening bolt searching for her sister's. Lucy focused her thoughts on the far side of the pond, the spot near the reeds where the pretty orange fish liked to hide. Off to her left she could hear Lily struggling and her sniffling as she began to cry. "Please, Lucy....." she begged silently, but Lucy decided to ignore her for a little while longer. Lily needed to learn that Lucy was the oldest, by three and a half minutes anyhow, and that she was in charge.

Unfortunately, Lily's mewling was even more annoying than the humming. She let herself glide back to her sister and wound her fingers through Lily's. For a while both girls were silent. Overhead, an owl swooped down low, crying in the night. Shortly there was the brief scream as it captured a tiny vole near the base of the Japanese maple. Lucy imagined the owl ripping out the vole's throat, the hot, red blood spilling on the white stones beneath the tiny tree.

"I'm cold," Lily said. She said it aloud this time, instead of thinking it. Aloud her voice was rasping and ugly, totally unlike the sweet, babyish voice Lucy could hear when they spoke mind to mind. She wondered briefly what her own voice would sound like if she tried speaking. Would it sound like Lily's? Like that of an old, old woman?

"I know, sister," Lucy thought gently. She stroked Lily's hand with one finger. It seemed to calm her sibling. They floated like that for a while, maybe hours or maybe seconds or even weeks. Time meant nothing to them anymore.

Beneath them, the clock ticked softly. They were so used to the rhythm of it that they barely heard it anymore.

"Will she help us?" Lily asked.

Lucy sighed. Above her a star shot across the indigo sky. "There are no secrets that time will not reveal," she whispered.

"But - she will help us?"

"Yes," Lucy thought. "Yes, sister, she will. She must."

8

Nora awoke to the feeling of chill rain on her cheek and the fuzzy sounds of weeping, the muffled squawk of a police radio and

Lucien's voice in her ear. She opened her eyes slowly, wincing at the pain in her temple. "Hold still, m'am," said a woman paramedic at her left. She was applying pressure to Nora's head with a square of gauze. At her right, Lucien leaned in.

"There you are," he said gently.

Nora was struck, as she always was, at his rugged good looks. Worry played around his eyes as he spoke. His hair was damp from the misty rain. Around them colored lights from two ambulances and a police car pulsed in the night.

"What happened?" Nora said groggily.

"I was going to ask you that," Lucien replied.

"Sir, we're ready to roll," the paramedic said to Lucien.

"Roll?" Nora said, trying to sit up, the pain in her head increasing.

"Hold on," Lucien said, he and the paramedic reaching for her at the same time and easing her back down onto the gurney.

"We're taking you to the hospital," the paramedic said. "You need that head wound checked out."

"Head wound?" Nora blinked. What the hell had happened?

"I'll ride along," Lucien said.

"No-" Nora said. "No- no hospital. I-" She turned then, as another gurney rolled past her moving toward the second ambulance, two paramedics trailing, one talking hurriedly into his radio and the other holding an IV bag aloft. Doris Waldemar trailed stoically behind holding the arm of Vivian, who was sobbing.

"What happened?" Nora asked Lucien.

"Heart attack," Lucien replied. "What the hell happened in there? Kat said there was some kind of weird power failure or something?"

What had happened? Nora tried to think, the pain in her head increasing. The black out...the twins. She shuddered.

"We need to load her, sir," the paramedic said, giving Nora a worried glance. She taped a fresh square of gauze to Nora's forehead.

'No!" Nora said. "Wait!" She sat up quickly, ignoring the pain in her head, and at the same time Lucien's and the paramedic's hands shot out grasping Nora by the wrists. When their chilled hands touched her skin, it came back to her in a rush, the flickering lights, the crashing clock, and the twins' death grip on her arms. *There are no secrets time does not reveal.* Suddenly, her head was swimming again, blackness threatening the edges of her vision. She felt the gurney being lifted into the ambulance and saw Lucien climbing in, taking a seat at her head. Her stomach felt swoopy again, and she turned her head aside as she began to retch.

"Looks like a concussion," she heard the paramedic say and then Nora proceeded to black out into unconsciousness, Lucien's hand on her shoulder.

A familiar clucking woke her, and Nora opened her eyes to find she was in the hospital emergency room, Bernie on one side of the bed and Aunt Bobbi on the other talking softly to one another.

"Where's – where's Lucien?" were the first words out of Nora's mouth, and she noticed her grandmother and great-aunt give one another a knowing look. "No," she said. "It's not like that – I mean – he was with me. In the ambulance."

"He had to go," Aunt Bobbi said, "But he wanted us to tell you–"

"You took a nasty fall and cracked your head open," Bernie interrupted, shooting her sister a sharp look. "But the doc says you're going to be fine."

"Sister – " Bobbi said.

"If he wanted to say something he should have stuck around!" Bernie huffed. "But we all know Lucien sucks at that!"

"Bernie, stop it," Nora said wearily.

"Well," Bernie continued stubbornly. "He should have." Nora's grandmother hadn't made any secret of how she felt about Nora and Lucien divorcing. She thought Nora's story of the split being amicable was a load of crap and she didn't mind saying so every chance she got. She saw Lucien as someone who'd hurt Nora, and she just couldn't forgive him that.

"We should tell her about her–" Bobbi insisted.

"She can see for herself," Bernie said. "She should. It's better that way."

"See what?" Nora asked. She found the controls on the bed rail and sat herself up. For a moment, the room swam a little, but then her vision cleared. She gingerly reached up and felt the bandage on her forehead.

Bobbi opened her mouth to speak, but Nora saw her grandmother shoot her aunt a warning look. " Uh - four stitches," said Aunt Bobbi.

"And you're staying overnight," Bernie said.

"For observation," Aunt Bobbi added.

"No," Nora said, swinging her legs over the side of the bed. "I'm fine and I'll-"

"Stay right where you are," said a young doctor as he entered the room. He walked over and held his hand out to Nora. "I'm Doctor Stein," he said. "You have a slight concussion and we want to keep an eye on you overnight."

"No, really I –" Nora began.

"Just to be on the safe side, Ms. Pepper." He saw the look of protest on Nora's face and sighed. "Look, would it help if I told you I'm a friend of Lucien's? And I promised him I'd keep you overnight and make sure-"

"She'll stay," Bernie said, patting Nora's hand. "Not because Lucien says so." She narrowed her eyes at Doctor Stein. "But because I do."

Doctor Stein shined a light in Nora's eyes, asked her to squeeze his fingers and then asked her some inane questions, such as the date, whether she knew where she was, who the president was. After telling her they would monitor her overnight, he left the room.

Beside the bed, Bobbi had taken a small hand mirror out of her purse. "Show her," she said to Bernie.

"Better, I'd guess," Bernie said. She approached Nora and held the mirror to her face. Nora gasped as she saw that one curly strand of her black hair had gone completely white.

9

Nora tried to calm her impatience and anxiety by flipping through the television channels from her hospital bed, thinking that some inane daytime television program might take her mind off...well, the things she didn't want to think about. The party. What she'd seen and heard. And...Lucien. She'd already been poked and prodded, had reluctantly forced down the bland, mushy breakfast that had been served to her at the crack of dawn, Now she was waiting for Doctor Stein to come in and discharge her so she could go home and have a proper shower and call Kat about their schedule that week. Finally giving up on finding anything worth watching, Nora tossed the remote aside, reached for her bag, which was lying on the bedside table and began digging in it. Near the bottom she rescued a small, round compact, and after fishing it out, opened it up and held it up to her face. There was a bandage taped to her temple, but except for that, she looked better than she'd anticipated. A bit tired, perhaps – trying to get sleep in the hospital was pretty futile- but no worse for the wear. Her hair, though, that was a different story. The wiry, springy curls were a rat's nest and Nora began to comb through it with her fingers trying to get some kind of control. And the white streak – how had that happened?

There was a soft chuckle from the doorway. "It's not that bad." He noted the streak in her hair and brushed at his own graying temples. "Guess we're all getting a little older, hey?"

Nora clutched the blankets to her chest and turned to see Daniel Spruce holding a small bouquet of miniature purple iris and daisies. "I remember you liked these?" he said, coming hesitantly into the room and placing the small, ceramic container on her bedside table.

"Daniel – " Nora's tongue felt thick and dry. "What – what are you doing here?"

His face colored slightly. "I know – we're not exactly – I mean, we haven't – " He shifted from foot to foot and stuck a nervous hand in his trouser pocket. "I wanted to make sure you were all right," he said. "After last night. I was here anyway – with Vivian – her grandfather – he -."

Nora sat up and pulled the sheets tighter around her. "That was nice of you," she said. "I'm fine. Really. Just – waiting to go home, actually."

An uncomfortable silence filled the room. Daniel looked out the window. "How – how is Mister Waldemar?" Nora asked.

"Not good," Daniel replied. "He had emergency cardiac surgery last night. He's in the ICU. We're not sure he's going to make it."

"I'm sorry to hear it," Nora said. The small talk felt stiff and uncomfortable. She wanted nothing more than for Daniel Spruce to leave. She hadn't been alone in a room with him for more than fifteen years. "Well…" she said, but he didn't say anything, just continued staring out at the beautiful, spring day. "And how's Vivian?" Nora asked, hating herself for continuing the conversation. Didn't he realize she was uncomfortable? That seeing him brought back all her high school embarrassment and humiliation in a rush? The betrayal of her best friend and the boy she'd been in love with? He probably didn't, she thought to herself. Daniel Spruce had never been very astute at picking up on social cues. To say the least. And looking at him now – yes, he was very good looking. But he didn't seem to have much substance.

"She's – " He looked at Nora helplessly, then gave her a half smile. "She's Vivian." He cleared his throat. "Well, I guess I'd better get back– " he jabbed a thumb toward the door.

"Sure," Nora said, brushing her hand over her hair again.

Daniel smiled. "It really isn't that bad," he said. "I always did like your wild hair."

Nora smiled uncomfortably. Her throat felt tight. "Yes – well-"

"Right," Daniel said. "I'll just –" He turned toward the door and took a step toward the hall, colliding directly with Lucien who was striding in. Nora bit her lip when she saw that he, too, was carrying an identical vase of purple irises and daisies. Some of the water from the vase lapped out as the two men crashed into one another, spilling onto the lapel of Daniel Spruce's jacket.

"Spruce," Lucien said, stiffly, stepping back.

"Detective," Daniel said, brushing at his jacket with his fingers. "Sorry – I was – ah – just going."

"Indeed," said Lucien.

Daniel raised a hand weakly to Nora. "Feel better," he said and slipped quickly out into the hall.

"What the hell was that?" Lucien asked giving the identical vase of flowers Daniel had left an offending look as he set his down. He smirked. "Got here before me, I see," he said. "Again."

Nora lay back on her pillow. "Knock it off, Lucien," she said.

"Okay, okay, I didn't come here to fight. Don't be so damned sensitive. We all did dumb stuff when we were in high school. And Spruce was definitely -" He sat on the edge of her bed, a too familiar feeling that made Nora tighten up.

She gave him a sharp look. "Do you mind?" she asked.

He grinned. "Gotcha," he said. He rose and moved to the window. "Nice day."

"And?" Nora had had enough small talk with Daniel Spruce.

"I was going to ask how you were feeling," Lucien said. "But I can see that for myself." He grinned. Nora rolled her eyes. "How are you feeling?" he asked after a beat.

"Fine," she said. "I want to get out of here."

"What does Stein say?"

"Nothing, yet," Nora said impatiently. "He hasn't been in yet."

Lucien headed for the door. "I'll see if I can round him up for you."

"Lucien – wait – " Nora blew out a frustrated breath. He was already out and down the hall. Lucien always had to fix things. Right now. Immediately. It was one of the things about him that drove her crazy – and that she liked about him, if she were to admit it. It had been tough learning to do things for herself – everything, in fact, after the divorce. But it had been empowering, too, learning that she was stronger – and smarter – that she realized she was. Not that he'd ever tried to make her dependent on him – she'd done that hadn't she? Hadn't it been easy just to let him? But now she knew she didn't need Lucien to take care of her, and she resented the fact that he'd jumped in to do just that without bothering to ask her what she wanted or let her do what was needed herself. However, when he came back within ten minutes with a red-faced Doctor Stein who examined her quickly and agreed to release her immediately, she had to admit she was the teeniest bit grateful. He'd also offered to drive her home, and not wanting to disturb Kat who was holding down the fort at The Pepper Pot, Nora agreed.

Outside the day was fresh and warm and full of summer promise. Nora rolled down the window and the breeze caught in her already disastrous hair, the soft ringlets creating a cyclone around her head. She reached into her bag and pulled out one of her scarves, this one silk with swirls of green and aqua and purple and tied it around her unruly locks. She put her head back against the seat and let the sunshine sink into her skin.

"I hate the hospital," she said, closing her eyes.

Lucien sighed. "I know," he said. Nora was thinking about the last time she was there, seven years ago. The night her father died. Ever since then, she couldn't stand being within its red brick walls.

Nora opened her eyes and watched the houses go by, the clapboard and brick and vinyl sided homes that made up the small town of Ashton Bay, yards with beds of spring flowers and quaint yard gnomes and cement deer and angels. It was a nice community, a community of people who were generally nice and helped one another. It lay on the north and south banks of the Archambault River, an old logging town whose north and south sides connected by three bridges. As Lucien's car headed over the Old East Bridge, Nora looked out at the river, the water below sparking like diamonds. She thought about the hundreds of times she'd ridden alongside Lucien on spring days just like this one and suddenly felt a hitch in her chest. She sat up straighter and took a deep breath, willing the unwanted feeling away. She blamed it on her exhaustion, the pain in her head and suddenly wanted nothing more that to be out of the car and home in her apartment. Alone.

"Where are we going?" she said as she sat up, noticing Lucien had taken a wrong turn and was headed away from The Pepper Pot and the apartment she lived in above it.

"Bernie called me," he said, his mouth tightening.

Nora leaned toward Lucien. "No," she said. "Absolutely not. Lucien, you turn this car around right now. I don't want to go to Bernie's. I want to go home."

"Can't," he said, not looking at her. "Promised." He glanced at Nora as she huffed out a frustrated breath. "And I have to say," he continued. "I agree with her for once."

"Of course you do," Nora said angrily under her breath, turning her head away from him. Why did this man have to be so maddening?

<u>10</u>

Despite her protests, Nora had to admit it was nice to be at Bernie and Bobbi's little cottage nestled on a wooded lot at the edge of a tributary of the Archambault River. The property had been in the Pepper family for decades, though the main house, which had been located near front of the acreage on River Road, had long since burned to the ground. The barn was still standing on the front lot, however, and Bernie had refurbished it as her pottery studio and shop, Mystic Clay. The barn was surrounded by wild herb and flower gardens, stone paths and fruit trees, and it was on these magical grounds that Nora had spent much of her childhood and where her father, Charlie Pepper, had grown up.

The cottage was located further back in the woods, right at the edge of the river, and had been the old Pepper hunting cabin. Since moving in to the cottage with her lover, Chance Delacoix in the 1950s, Bernie had added on some rooms, a metal roof, and a large, screened porch that faced the trees and the river. It was complete with a large, black iron pot-bellied stove that had been rescued from the old house. In the wintertime, Bernie snapped in the custom-made windows over the screens and when the stove was lit, the porch was a magical place. It was furnished with old, bentwood chairs and a chaise, patch quilts and homemade decorations of shell and stone and bone and branch. It was Nora's favorite place in the cottage, and it was here that her grandmother had settled her, covered with the old, blue quilt she liked best, a mug of sweet tea in her hand.

Nora had claimed the chaise and Bobbi sat across from her in a large, padded rocking chair. She had her feet up on a squat upholstered stool and was reading, which was her favorite pastime. They were both relaxing while Bernie spent her morning, as was her custom, in her pottery studio building the platters and trays and bowls she was well known for. It had already warmed enough to have the porch opened up, and a warm breeze wafted through, gently moving the wind chimes which tinkled softly. The tinkling reminded Nora of what had happened in the kitchen of the Waldemar house – the sudden wind, the chimes, the twin girls standing at the edge of the ruined pond. She understood now why the lawn man hadn't seen them – they hadn't been there, not really. But she'd been able to see them. And that was something Nora definitely didn't want to think about.

She took a swallow of her tea and cleared her throat. "Bobbi?"

Her great-aunt looked up from her book and cocked an eyebrow.

"Remember when I was little and I was having – all those – those dreams?"

"The precognitions you mean," Bobbi said. She closed the book and put it down in her lap.

"No," Nora said nervously. "They were – dreams. Dreams that- um –"

"Foretold the future?" Bobbi said pointedly. "Helped you find something that was missing? Gave you a message from-"

"Stop!" Nora said. "You know I don't believe in all that stuff. I-"

"Don't you?" Bobbi asked.

Nora looked into her great aunt's eyes. She knows, Nora thought. "No! Yes. I don't know." Nora set her teacup down with a clink, spilling some of the liquid onto the saucer. She pulled the quilt up as if it were a shield. Bobbi looked at her gently. "I don't *want* to anyhow," Nora said finally.

"I know, dear," Bobbi said. "I really wish you weren't so afraid.

They were both silent for a moment. Outside a band of chickadees attacked the chipped ceramic bowl of seeds and grains Bernie had left for them. She had her "foo-pees" as she called them, always charmingly mispronouncing *faux pas*. Nora had corrected her many times, but to Bernie, they were still foo-pees. She had placed them all over the property – bowls and platters that had cracked during firing, or had somehow gone wrong. She used them to feed the wildlife, birds and squirrels and foxes – offerings, she called them, though Nora preferred to think of the act simply as a cute little-old-lady thing to do; feeding the birds. Bobbi looked at Nora and sighed. She picked up the book she was reading. *Angel Island.*

"What was that for?" Nora asked.

"What, dear?" She looked at Nora a bit impatiently over the tops of her reading glasses.

"The dramatic sigh."

"Oh," Bobbi smiled. "It's nothing, dear."

"Right," said Nora under her breath. She watched the birds for a few more moments. She loved their chattering and antics. The chickadees were her favorites, and when she was a little girl, she used to sit outside on the stump of the old pine watching them and sometimes even feeding them out of her palm. She thought they were her pets. "Remember when you and Bernie made me the dream pillow?" she asked.

Bobbi chuckled. "That old thing?" she said. "That wasn't anything. We told you it was magic, but it was just an old cushion from the attic."

"But it made the dreams stop," Nora protested.

"No, it didn't," Bobbi said without looking up from her book. "We'd never do that. You did that. You made them stop."

Nora chewed on her bottom lip. "It's happening again," she said.

Across the room, Bobbi sighed. "I know, dear," she said. "We've always known it would. For a long time. Things like this – well, you just can't stop them."

"It's worse now," Nora said. "Not just dreams. I mean, I'm awake now – when I – see things."

Bobbi broke out into a gummy smile. "Congratulations, dear!" she said and then stubbornly went back to her reading.

Nora sat back on the chaise and pulled the quilt closer. She should have foreseen that reaction, she thought. Her grandmother and great-aunt had never been reticent about Nora's "gifts" as they called them. In fact, they constantly encouraged her to embrace them. But Nora wanted nothing to do with that. She'd had a lifetime of whispering and gossip about her grandmother and her aunt, the alleged 'witches of the Archambault Woods', and she didn't like or want to be associated with that.

Her mother had instilled that in her as well, she guessed, her dismissal of the paranormal. Ivy Barrett-Pepper had wanted nothing to do with her mother-in-law and kooky (as she called her) sister and their weird tarot-reading, herb-growing, moon gazing ways. And she definitely didn't want her daughter acting like them. Aside from that, if Nora admitted it to herself, all that stuff made her nervous, maybe even scared her a bit. And she didn't want to think about it right now. She'd promised Kat she would take the day off and rest and that was something she didn't do often. Maybe she'd find a good book, take a cue from Bobbi and read a little.

She sat up and swung around on the chaise so she could face the bookshelf that was built into the wall below the window. As she bent and perused the eclectic selection of books, a shudder suddenly ran through her and she felt an icy coldness creep into her belly once again. The room spun as she remembered the feeling of the twins' cold fingers on her wrists, the sound of the ticking clock with its huge, brass pendulum swinging back and forth. As she ran her fingers over the spines of the books she remembered where she had seen the twins before – or at least girls that looked exactly like the twins. She reached out and snatched the old photo album off the shelf and hurriedly turned the pages until she came to the old, sepia photograph she was searching for. There on the page was the photo of the Pepper sisters, her grandmother, Bernice and her sisters, Roberta and Elizabeth. Bernie, Bobbi and Bettie Pepper. In the photograph they were ages two, eight and fourteen, respectively, their faces were mirror images of those of the ghost twins.

11

Bernie Pepper had suffered her share of grief and loss. In 1937, when Bernie was just six years old, her oldest sister, Bettie went missing at age seventeen. Bettie had been like a mother to Bernie, and she'd felt her loss deeply. No one knew how or why or where she'd gone, whether she'd been taken or had run away, even whether she was alive or dead, though Bernie was fairly certain it was the latter. One day her beloved Bettie was simply – gone. And they'd never seen nor heard from her again.

Bernie worked the mound of clay beneath her strong hands, kneading, making sure to release any air bubbles that were trapped within the malleable substance. Air bubbles were like tiny bombs within the clay and could cause a piece to crack, split, and even explode during the firing process. The kneading always took a long time, but Bernie didn't mind. It was one of her favorite parts of the process. At least it was now. It required patience, determination, and stamina. For Bernie it was also somewhat therapeutic - working the cool clay made her think of the people she'd lost, people she believed had gone back to the earth from which the clay came. Touching the clay was like touching them, somehow, creating out it was a way of honoring their stories and memories – especially those of Chance Delacoix, the first love of her life, and their son, Charlie, the most precious love of her life, second only to her granddaughter, Nora, who reminded her in so many ways of her only child.

Bernie thought of Charlie every day, even though he'd been gone more than seven years. And it was no secret that she blamed Nora's mother, Ivy, in part, for his death. The car crash had been sudden and fatal, precipitated by a horrible argument between Nora's parents when Charlie discovered that Ivy had been having an affair – with the very man she was now married to, Tom Bell. He was a nice enough man, charming, quiet and intelligent, but Bernie could not help holding a grudge, and neither could Nora. Tom had done his best to try to mend the rift between them, but Pepper women were stubborn – and Ivy was as well. And so, mother and daughter remained estranged.

Bernie lost Chase soon after Charlie died. But then, she'd lost Chase over and over during the tumultuous forty plus years they'd spent together. Chase had been an old hippie, a gypsy, a wanderer, and an artist. It was because of him that she'd found her own calling as a potter and artist, because of his encouragement, his love for her – even the fact that he'd left her several times during their long relationship, time when he pursued his own creative dreams and Bernie used the time to stretch her artist's wings to fill the days and weeks of loneliness. His legacy to her was the studio he'd build in the old barn, and the upper level still held in its heart the large, open loft in which he used to paint, and the lower one Bernie's ceramics studio. Yes, she'd spent a lot of her life missing him. And while she'd been lonely sometimes, angry sometimes, it had made her independent – after she'd gotten it through her head that Chase would always come back to her, no matter what. But he was often "on the road", as he called it, just like the book by Kerouac, creating, fighting causes, building sculptures, painting murals, feeding disabled veterans – or simply "experiencing life."

There were times Bernie thought she hated him, times when money was slim or when Charlie passed some milestone or just needed his daddy. But Chase always came back – and when he was there, ensconced in the magical, little cottage they shared, life was so very good that the times she was on her own didn't seem to faze her anymore as the years went by. Her non-traditional relationship was the root of much gossip in the small town of Ashton Bay, but Bernie didn't care one fig about that. After Charlie died, Chase had come home from the Arizona desert broken and silent. He'd quickly withered away, just sitting on the screened porch staring out at the woods. He'd barely eaten or talked. He stopped laughing, playing his guitar and driving his beloved Jeep. Barely three months after Charlie died, Chase was gone, too. Aggressive cancer, the doctors said, but Bernie knew that the real cause was a broken heart. Love, she thought, had so many ways to hurt a body.

For a while after her beloved son and lover passed, Bernie stopped working in her studio. Being there reminded her too much of Chase, too much of Charlie. She sat in the cottage for days on end, in Chase's overstuffed chair on the screen porch, sitting exactly where he'd sat, mourning their son. She ignored the telephone, her customers, and her sister – even Nora, to a degree. It was just too hard to look at her, her face reminded Bernie too much of her only son. Inside, Bernie had felt awful. She knew that Nora needed her right then just as much as she needed Nora – but she just couldn't seem to pull herself out.

Then one late autumn day, she'd been sitting on the screen porch. It had been chilly, but she hadn't been able to make herself put the windows back up over the screens yet. She hadn't been doing much of anything, and the cottage was cloaked in a layer of dust and cobwebs. She was barely eating, and she'd lost a good deal of weight. Through the screen, she suddenly heard some loud crashing, coming from the direction of the barn studio. It was a still day, with no breeze, and the sound carried clearly. When the crashing didn't let up, Bernie knew she had to get up and investigate. Outside, the crashing was louder and insistent. She jogged toward the barn and as she came up upon it, saw that the huge doors were thrown open and there was her sister, Bobbi, heaving green ware Bernie hadn't gotten around to glazing out the door, smashing it in the barnyard.

She was also crying, her face red and chest heaving.

Bernie, completely out of breath, leaned on her knees, wheezing. She was almost seventy, after all, as was her sister. "What the hell are you doing?" she yelled. "Stop that!"

Bobbi looked at Bernie stubbornly. "No!" she yelled back and heaved a bowl at her sister. It barely missed Bernie's knee and smashed into pieces at her feet. "What good is any of this stuff if you're going to let it all rot!"

"Clay doesn't rot!" Bernie yelled back nonsensically.

"Well, you do! You are! You're just sitting in that house! Rotting!" And then Bobbi's face had gone white, and she'd collapsed backward on the barn floor, clutching a green ware platter.

After that incident, and nearly losing her sister as well, Bernie made her way back to her life. She'd moved Bobbi in with her, and the two sisters had lived together ever since. They laughed now, sometimes, about the spectacle of the two of them in the barnyard that day, broken pottery lying around them, two ancient ladies fighting like children. Bernie pushed the lump of clay down again and began molding it into a large square. She was fairly certain it was bubble-free and ready to use. She was planning on building another large platter, like the one she'd given her granddaughter, only square-ish this time, glazed black with spirals etched in the edges. She could see it in her mind when she looked at the mound of clay, and that sight made her feel content, happy.

Suddenly, there was a jangling coming from the cottage. It was the large bell she and Bobbi had hung at the front door. They used it as a signal – and the way it was ringing, it sounded as if her sister was distressed. Bernie wiped her hands on her shirt and headed quickly out the door. She hopped on her bicycle and pedaled, as quickly as she could, down the lane toward the cabin in the woods.

12

Doris Waldemar sat on the hospital's board of directors but disliked, intensely, being inside the hospital proper. The boardroom, located on the hospital's topmost floor, was like another land – it was safe, free from commotion and germs and patients. Here, in the intensive care unit, the lights were too bright, machines beeped and sighed, and patients moaned. She sat stiffly on the uncomfortable chair near Glenn's bedside, staring at his waxy-looking face. He was still in and out of consciousness, after nearly three days, and Doris was getting impatient. Glenn was weak, he always had been, letting any kind of illness or ache keep him down. Yes, yes, she knew that this time it was serious, a heart attack and the resulting cardiac surgery – but she needed him to wake up and pull himself together so she could get out of here – get him out of here, she corrected herself – and transferred to the small, exclusive rehabilitation facility where they were both donors and chaired the board. The Valley-Green Memorial Center was clean. It was dignified and lushly appointed. The staff moved quietly through the halls to the private rooms. Doris had wanted Glenn transferred immediately, more for herself, truth be told, but his cardiac surgeon wouldn't hear of it, she'd said, until Glenn was more stable.

Beside her, Glenn moaned and shifted in the bed, his face twisting into a grimace. Near him, the monitor by the bedside beeped a warning, and within seconds a nurse in aqua scrubs was at his bedside checking it and him.

"What is it?" Doris asked the nurse, who ignored her and put a hand on Glenn's chest.

"Mister Waldemar?" she said. "Glenn? How are you doing, sir?" She put two fingers on his wrist and consulted her watch.

Glenn moaned again and his eyelids fluttered. His mouth opened between dry, cracked lips. When he opened his eyes, they were somewhat cloudy, and, Doris could see, welling with tears. "Did you see them?" he rasped, clutching at the air, searching for her hand. "Did you see the girls?"

13

When Bernie burst in the cottage door, she saw Bobbi and Nora on the sun porch, clutching a book between them. Bobbi was crying and Nora was sitting on the footstool at her feet, holding her great-aunt's hand with one of hers and a book she was balancing on her knees with the other. It was one of the old albums, open to a page of sepia-colored photographs. When Bernie stepped into the cozy sunroom, her sister and granddaughter looked up at her at the same time, and Bernie could not help the instant, almost seasick feeling she got in her stomach at the look on her sister's face. "What is it?" Her voice was a whisper. Around her, the room felt like it was full of cotton that surrounded her, cutting off her breath and making her knees suddenly weak. She'd had this feeling many times before and she recognized it. The feeling of *knowing*. Of something about to happen.

Bobbi's mouth moved, but at first nothing would come out. A single tear leaked down her wrinkled cheek. "It's Bettie," she said finally. "I think Nora has seen Bettie."

The three women stared at one another, time suspended. Bernie took a step forward, her eyes focused on the photo album, the picture of herself and her two sisters. Bernie could almost remember the day it had been taken. It had been the Fourth of July. She was just six years old and the Pepper family had been enjoying a picnic outside. Fried chicken and corn on the cob and cold potato salad. And ice cream, they'd made it together, all three girls taking a turn at turning the handle on the churn while Daddy salted the big chunks of ice that surrounded the canister.

This had happened before the main house burned, and the wide, white gingerbread porch could be seen in the background. The three sisters were sitting on the ground on a checkered cloth wearing identical dresses. Bernie seemed to recall they were a pale shade of blue, with short, puffy sleeves and round necklines. Beneath Bettie's bodice were tiny bumps that bespoke her impending womanhood. Bernie was in Bettie's lap, and Bobbi sat next to her, her head lay adoringly on her big sister's shoulder. Their granny used to call them the three peas in a pod; they were so close, despite their difference in ages.

"What – " Bernie started, and then there was a loud knocking at the door. All three heads turned toward it, the atmosphere in the room changing suddenly as they did so, a movement, leaking and swirling, like water draining from a bathtub. It was lighter, normalcy returned. Between Nora and Bobbi, the album fell to the floor, its pages closing. They all looked down at it for a moment, mouths open. The knocking grew louder and more insistent. "It's probably – uh – it's Stewart, I expect," said Bernie distractedly, heading toward the door.

Nora turned to her great-aunt. "Stewart?" she asked. "You mean-"

Bobbi's eyes were still somewhat clouded. "Yes," she said. "Stewart Schmidt. The ghost hunter."

14

Stewart Schmidt had been friends with the old Pepper sisters for about two years before he'd founded his paranormal examinations company, Spectral Investigations in 2010. The business had been a struggle, to say the least, but being friends with the Pepper sisters, rumored to be adept hands at divination, dream analysis and even precognition, gave him a little credibility, anyhow, with the set who believed in such things. Even the small city's government had given him some irritating troubles when he launched his business, forcing him to pay six hundred dollars for a business license – it was the same fee they forced tarot card readers, massage therapists, and alternative medicine practitioners – or any business owner, for that matter, whose business description didn't fit the "norm". It was a small town mentality that Stew abhorred, but he liked living in Ashton Bay, which was rife with old buildings and houses and Native American burial grounds – places that made it possible to carry out his work without having to go too far afield. Bernie and Bobbi Pepper didn't exactly understand his scientific approach to the spirit world; they'd been supportive and almost motherly. It was frustrating, at times, having them cluck over his analyses like they were cute drawings made by a kindergartener, but for the most part, he'd learned a lot from them. He hoped that they learned some new things from him as well.

He'd been excited to learn that Bernie's granddaughter, Nora, was with them at the cottage for the day. He'd been calling The Pepper Pot and leaving messages since learning the evening before about the events that had taken place at the Waldemar estate. That morning he'd gotten Kat Kalinowski on the phone who'd asked him to please not call again – that Nora was off for the day. He'd cringed at her impatient tone. While he knew Kat was an occasional tarot customer of Bobbi Pepper, Stewart knew that she was probably one of the people in town who thought that he was a complete fake, laughable, even. He remembered the school-boy crush he'd had on her in seventh grade, and her imagined distain of him felt all the more hurtful.

Oh, who cared about that anymore, he thought. After overhearing a conversation in Jake's Corner Bar between two of the part time servers who worked for Nora and Kat the evening after the

Waldemars' anniversary party, Stew had been hot to talk with Nora Pepper and find out exactly what had happened that night. Flickering lights? Weird sounds? He wondered if there had been any EVP's and was mad to get his equipment in there. And the Waldemar estate, no less – it had to be at least one hundred and fifty years old and jam-packed with spirit activity. He'd give his eyeteeth to check that place out. All he needed was an in – and he thought Nora might be just that. He had, of course, tried calling the Waldemar estate directly, but that had been a definite brick wall. Now, he figured, considering his friendship with Bernie and Bobbi, Nora Pepper might be amenable to speaking with him.

When Bernie let him in she looked distracted and didn't offer him a cup of her delicious herbal tea as she usually did. Her short, snow-white hair was disheveled, and her glasses hung askew on the chain around her neck. "Come on," was all she said, leading him through the cottage and out onto the sun porch. There, Stew saw Bobbi sitting in her favorite rocker, and Nora Pepper sitting on an ottoman at her feet. There was an old photo album on her lap. She cocked a disapproving eyebrow at Stewart. He'd run into her on occasion before, when he was visiting the Pepper sisters and knew well what she thought of him – or more accurately what he did for a living. Well, it was sort of a living. Okay, so he lived in his mom's basement – and he had to work part time at Radio Shack – but hey, once things got off the ground…

"I think we have a bony-fide case for you," Bobbi said as he sat on the edge of the chaise.

"What?" Nora said. She looked from her aunt to her grandmother and back again. "Are you kidding?"

"No, dear," Bobbi said. "Stewart is an investigator."

"Paranormal investigator," Stew corrected.

"Oh, that's just bull-" Nora sputtered.

"Nora," Bernie interrupted. "Don't be stubborn. You said yourself-"

"I don't want to talk about that with a – " she stopped herself short and looked at Stewart, her face reddening. "Stranger."

"Well, Steward is not a stranger to us," Bobbi said. "And if we can find Bettie-"

"Who's Bettie?" Stewart asked. The atmosphere in the room was charged. He could feel that without any of his equipment, his digital voice recorders and motion detectors and EMF. Something was happening with the Peppers – something that had to do with the incident at the Waldemar estate, he was sure of it – and Stewart was just about to be let in on it. If Nora Pepper didn't get in the way, that was. Bernie and Bobbi had confided in him on more that one occasion just how Nora felt about spirits and messages and readings. She wanted nothing to do with any of it, much to her grandmother and great-aunt's chagrin.

"Bettie is – was – our sister," Bobbi said.

"Our oldest sister," Bernie added.

"She disappeared," Bobbi said. "In 1937. And now, Nora's seen her."

"No!" said Nora. "I – didn't I – "

55

Stewart shoulders hunched disappointedly. "Oh," he said. "I thought this had to do with the incident at the Waldemars' anniversary party."

"It does," Bernie said, sitting beside Stewart on the chaise.

"That's where she saw her," Bobbi continued.

"And look what happened to her," Bernie said, pointing at Nora's head.

Nora had pulled her hair back into a sloppy bun, trying to hide the newly pure white streak, more so she didn't have to look at a reminder of that terrible night than anything else. As soon as she got back into town tomorrow, she planned on heading to Suzi's Salon to have it dyed black, but until then, she didn't want to think about it. Her hand went up self-consciously to her hair, simply drawing Stewart's attention there rather than repelling it.

"That happened last night?"

"Well, what do you think?" Nora said defensively. "I'm only thirty-two years old, after all!"

"Gramma Eulie Pepper went all gray at age thirty," Bobbi said.

"Not helping, Aunt Bobbi!" Nora said gruffly. Next to Stewart, Bernie snickered a little. Nora threw her a sharp glance. She stood. "Look," she said. "I'm going home. I don't want anything to do with-"

"Nora Pepper, you sit down this instant!" her grandmother said, and Nora did, out of instinct. It wasn't often in her life that

Bernie was sharp with her, but when she was, Nora had made sure she did as she was told.

"Bernie-" she began.

"Listen, miss," Bernie said. "I know what you think about all this, and I know how you feel." Suddenly her green eyes filled with tears. "But I want to tell you how I feel for a change. Bettie was my sister and I loved her." She looked at Bobbi. "We all did. And we've never known what happened to her. Now, I don't know what you saw or what you didn't see, but if there is the smallest chance that we can find our sister – well, Bobbi and I want to find her. And you're going to help us."

15

Vivian stood on her bedroom balcony, looking out at the gardens and the pond in dismay. Below her, the pretty orange koi that had been added for the party were, like the expensive Megalotis fish before them, floating dead on the water's glassy surface. Vivian didn't understand it. The lawn care man had tested the water and had found nothing out of the ordinary, and he'd tested the soil around the pond as well, but like the plants before them, all the new foliage was turning dark brown and gray and dying off. She remembered the morning she'd awoken, four days before the party. She'd taken her morning coffee out on the balcony and stood exactly where she was standing now and had looked down at the ruin that had occurred overnight – all the plants within a six-foot radius around the pond had been dead. Hydrangeas and grasses and moss that had been there for

57

years completely brown, right down to their roots, she'd found out later. The lawn care people said they had never seen anything like it and had worked overtime to replant the area in time for the party, as Vivian had demanded.

Now, it was all gone once again. Vivian sighed, and then shuddered. Something was going on here, no matter what her grandmother said – it was not Vivian's imagination. Something terrible was happening on the estate. At first, she'd had dreams. Odd dreams about floating in water. There was someone with her, holding her hand. As she floated, looking at the hazy moon and stars above, she remembered feeling odd, hollow almost, and cold. And there was a ticking, like a clock, she remembered that well. It had sounded exactly like the sound they'd heard the night of the party, and Vivian knew very well it wasn't the water system or the furnace or any other mechanical device in the old house. It was – something else. Something – that frightened her.

She'd seen things, too. Out of the corner of her eye. Shadows sometimes, that she could not explain, and when she saw them she felt as if she were no longer alone. She'd tried to shake it off. She'd never felt afraid in the big, old house, despite its drafty hallways and lofty rooms. It was exactly the type of house where you'd expect to find a good ghost story, but as far as she knew, the Waldemar family consisted of plain, normal folks – rich, perhaps – but with no family secrets. She'd thought about talking with Doris, but knew well what her grandmother would say. She was a prim, no-nonsense woman who had no used for fantasies. She'd roll her eyes and tell Vivian how ridiculous she was being.

Even after the party, after others beside Vivian had experienced the odd phenomena, and her grandfather, Glenn, had nearly been frightened to death, Doris had taken charge and called the plumbers and heating and cooling company and scheduled appointments. Vivian had to admit that since both companies had been in, there hadn't been any more odd sounds or flashing lights in the house – but the pond... What would Doris say about that? It wasn't Doris, Vivian decided as she gazed out at the gardens, that she wanted – needed - to talk to. It was her grandfather – he'd always been the one who would listen to her, comfort her, but he was ill and Vivian knew that right now, she had to keep her anxieties to herself.

16

Lucien Pike was always the voice of reason, and that was exactly what Nora felt she needed right now. He'd agreed to meet Nora at The Book Nook, a used book and coffee shop she'd always favored located in the quaint downtown area of Ashton Bay. It was a bit dusty, to be honest, but it was also cozy, quiet and smelled of baked goods and strong coffee, two of Nora's favorite smells in the whole world. The maze of shelves had been arranged into intimate alcoves where a person could read quietly, meet privately to chat, or just – think. Nora had settled herself into her favorite spot near the back of the shop where the shelves were lined with old cookbooks, gardening manuals and books about herbs and other edible plants. She was curled up in a dilapidated, brown upholstered chair, nursing a coffee laced with cinnamon. A fresh scone lay on a little, china plate on the table, untouched.

Nora had wrestled with herself a bit, albeit not as much as she liked to think she did, about calling Lucien. She needed to talk with someone who knew her intimately – knew the fears she wrestled with. Fears about herself. And that was something Lucien knew well. After all, it had been part of the reason they'd divorced. She didn't like feeling like she needed him or depended on him in any way since the divorce, but since they'd met, he'd been her closest confident – even closer than Kat Kalinowski who was like a little sister to Nora. There were things like this – highly personal things – that she felt more comfortable talking with him about than she did with anyone else. In part, because she knew that he thought a lot of the people who meant the most to her. Especially her grandmother, even though on the outside Bernie had held a grudge against Lucien since he and Nora had divorced. Inside, Nora knew that Bernie had and always would have, a soft spot for Lucien Pike, and when he and Nora had been together, she had doted on him almost as much as she had her son, Charlie.

Nora looked up as she heard the muted sound of the bell that hung on the front door of the bookshop. She tried to swallow down the butterflies she felt in her stomach at the thought of seeing Lucien. It was always like that, despite of the coolness she tried to show toward him. Being near him still made her feel like a school girl, fluttery and warm, and at the same time, there was a deep sense of peace, of home that she didn't seem to have anymore but felt whenever she was around him. She knew she had to get over it, just learn to be on her own once and for all – and for the most part, she was doing a good job of it. But sometimes…. Sometimes… her thoughts and feelings got the best of her. It had been like that after leaving Bernie and Bobbi's little cottage the night before. There had just been too much information for her to process, and now it was Lucien she needed to help her with that. Fair, intelligent, no nonsense Lucien. That he was so damned good looking was just a bonus in the deal.

He slid down into the chair across from her, a mug of black coffee in his hand. He was wearing a worn, gray corduroy jacket over a white button down shirt and blue jeans and his customary cowboy boots. His dark hair had gotten a little shaggy. Nora noticed a few silver strands at his temples but thought it suited him. He combed his fingers through his hair, pushing it back and took a drink of the strong coffee. He eyed her across the table.

"Stop staring," Nora said, her face coloring slightly under his gaze.

"Still can't get used to that," he said. His eyes were on her hair, and her hand went up self-consciously to the white strand that wound its way root to tip down the right side of her head.

"Try being me," she said. "I'm still freaked out every time I catch a glimpse of myself. I've got an appointment tomorrow afternoon. I'm going to have it dyed. Get rid of it."

Lucien shrugged. "I don't know," he said. "I kind of like it. Adds character."

"I need more character?" Nora snapped, cringing inside as she did so. Why did she always immediately go on the defensive with him?

Lucien grinned despite her tone. "Just saying," he replied. "Adds a certain – mystery."

"Great," Nora quipped. "Just what I need. More mystery."

"More?" He raised an eyebrow.

Nora set her cup down and scooted closer to the edge of her chair. "Bernie and Bobbi have been talking to me about their older sister."

"The one who went missing?"

"You know about that?"

"Sure," Lucien said. "Not too many cold cases like that one in Ashton Bay. The retired guys talk about it sometimes. She just vanished. Sixteen or seventeen years old, if I remember right? That's a lot for a family to deal with. Especially around here, farming community. Not too many runaways."

"Is that what you think? That she ran away?"

Lucien shrugged. "Maybe," he said. "I don't really know much about it. But if it were as simple as that she probably would have come back eventually. It wasn't like the Pepper family was an unhappy one, as far as I'm aware."

"That's what Bernie said," Nora replied. She chewed on her bottom lip and wound the newly white strand of hair around her finger, deep in thought. Lucien leaned toward her, his elbows on his knees.

"What's really bothering you?" he asked.

Nora took a deep breath. "You know how my grandmother is always talking to me about – my – gifts?" Lucien nodded. "Well," Nora continued. "I've been – seeing or experiencing – some – stuff." She could feel the heat in her face. She reached down and picked up her coffee and took a deep drink.

"What kind of stuff?" Lucien asked after a beat.

"Come on," Nora said. "You're supposed to laugh at me here and tell me how ridiculous that is."

"Oh, I don't know, " Lucien said. "Maybe it's ridiculous – maybe it's not."

"It *is* ridiculous." Nora sat back in the chair. "I'm just – maybe I'm just tired or something. Kat and I have been super busy and I-"

"I've been spending some time up North," Lucien interrupted. "Visiting relatives."

"What does that have to do with-"

"They're Ojibwe, you know," he continued. "On both sides. My mother's and father's people."

"Okay," Nora said, confused. "I knew that – " She shook her head. "Lucien, what does one thing have to do with another?"

"My mother's mother, my grandmother – they say she used to have these visions, dreams, that she could predict things that were going to happen-"

"Great," Nora said. "So we both have craziness in our families."

"Maybe it's not so crazy," Lucien said. "I know, I know," he held a hand up as Nora leaned forward about to protest. "I used to feel the same way you do. But, I've been listening to these stories. From my mother's relatives. Connection to – other worlds – is not far fetched in the culture." He sat back in his chair. "Listen. There are some stories my mother told me – things that can't be...rationally explained." He took a sip of his coffee, and then sat back and eyed Nora thoughtfully. "We had this case last year – remember that kid, Brian Derner? The one that went missing in the parking lot of the grocery store?"

"Right," Nora said. "I do remember. But you found him. He was taken by that janitor, the one who'd been fired from the school."

"Right," Lucien replied. "But do you know *how* I found him?"

Nora shrugged. "Amazing detective work?"

Lucien shook his head. "Your Aunt Bobbi," he said. "She had a vision. She told me exactly where that little boy was. And what happened to him."

Nora shook her head. "What? She never told me –"

"She didn't want any attention," he said. "She called me in confidence and I promised I'd keep what she told me a secret. She just wanted Brian back home safe with his family. And if I had blown her off like she was some kook, who knows what would have happened to that kid."

17

Vivian Waldemar-Spruce slammed the telephone down in frustration. For a change, she was glad that her grandmother, Doris, had insisted on keeping a landline in the house. It was so very satisfying to bang down a telephone receiver to end an upsetting call. She was at her wit's end with the lawn care company – and gossip being what it was in a small town, the other two companies she'd called refused to bid to work on the pond and surrounding area. Nothing in and around it would stay alive for more than three or four days. Every test that could be done of the soil and water had been performed and all appeared normal. There was just no rational reason why the area was now barren – after years and years of thriving.

Behind Vivian, standing in the doorway of the study, Doris Waldemar cleared her throat. Vivian turned. "What in the world is the problem?" Doris asked.

"It's the lawn company," Vivian said. "I'm at the end of my rope."

Doris walked across the room and poured herself a sherry. She sat, her back strong and straight even though she was in her eighties and regarded her granddaughter. "I told you what a huge responsibility the house and grounds would be," she said. "If you want me to take over again-"

"No!" Vivian said sharply. She shook her head to clear it, and then sat beside her grandmother on the divan. "Really. I can take care of it – they just – " her voice trailed off and she looked toward the window. "How's grandfather?"

Doris took a sip of her sherry. She sighed impatiently. "He should be home," she said. "But he's being – stubborn. You know how he can be."

Vivian looked at her feet. She rarely agreed with Doris about her grandfather. She always found him to be essentially sweet, though he often was a bit distracted, forgetful, almost as if he were always mentally elsewhere. But, she thought, he was getting older. That was to be expected. He'd been the one to nurture her when she was a child and her grandmother the one to discipline. They'd been her guardians since she was four and she lost her parents in a car accident in Germany. She and her mother had gone with her father on a business trip, accompanied by a nanny. One evening, after a cocktail party, her parents, probably both more than a little drunk, were driving back to the hotel and collided with a train. She'd been sent back to the United States to live with her grandparents. Vivian could barely remember her mother and father at all.

Vivian had always sensed a sadness about her grandfather, and she assumed it had to do with losing his only child. She also assumed that was what made him particularly tender toward her – and, she thought, that made Doris more than a little jealous. She'd always been so, as far back as Vivian could remember, and right now, even though she didn't agree with Doris, she preferred to remain silent – after all, she had to share the huge house with her alone until her grandfather and husband, who was away on an extended business trip, were back. It was not a prospect Vivian relished. Doris could be – quite overwhelming, to say the least.

"Well," she said. "Perhaps Grandfather can come home soon."

"Yes," Doris said, staring toward the fireplace. "If he can get over-" She stopped short, clamping her lips shut.

"What?" Vivian asked.

Doris was scowling. "He's afraid," she said, scowling. "How ridiculous!"

Vivian's thoughts traveled back to the night of the party, her grandfather's collapse. He *had* appeared afraid, she thought, but she had assumed it was because of the heart attack, his gasping breath. That had to have been a frightening feeling. Like drowning.

"It's perfectly natural for a person who's suffered a heart attack to be anxious about going home," Vivian said. "The thought that something like that could happen again-"

"It's not that!" Doris snipped. "He's afraid. To be in the house."

"But that's – " Vivian stopped. She was going to say *ridiculous*, mimicking her grandmother, but then she thought about the odd things that had been happening on the estate, the strange dreams she'd been having – at least she'd thought they were dreams. And the party – the flickering lights, the sounds – her grandfather staring and pointing into the hallway and then collapsing. What had he seen that had frightened him so? And then there was also the bane of Vivian's existence of late - the ring of death that surrounded the pond in the gardens. And she had to admit – she'd been feeling a little frightened herself. Anxious. As if something was happening she was unable to stop, like being on a ferris wheel at the mercy of the operator. And if Vivian had learned anything from Doris, it was that being in control was key. It was a place of comfort, of knowing what was happening.

As near as she could determine – and she'd been thinking about it quite a lot since the party – odd things had started happening about the same time she and Doris had begun planning the anniversary party at the end of winter. Things that seemed to vanish – or more to the point, seemed to be misplaced. The first item to go missing was Doris and Glenn's wedding album. She and Doris had been perusing it, choosing some photographs that perhaps they might like to enlarge to place on the mantle in the dining room for the party. Vivian had been sure they'd left it on the coffee table in the study, but when she'd gone back to find it, it had been gone. She'd looked everywhere, questioned her grandparents, but all that came of that was a good scolding from her grandmother over Vivian's apparent carelessness with Doris' things.

Other things pertaining to the party had come up missing as well: the guest list, which Vivian was forced to re-create with Doris' grudging assistance, subjecting her to more scolding.

Also missing were the silver pickle forks, which had always been in the same place in the credenza in the dining room, the key to the liquor cabinet and Doris' prized address book which had the contact information of "absolutely everybody." For a while, Vivian suspected Glenn of hiding things, that perhaps he wasn't keen on so much hoopla for the anniversary celebration. He'd been more distracted than usual, and looked as if he hadn't been sleeping well. Doris was harder on him than usual, so much so, in fact that Vivian had joked with her grandmother that she hoped they wouldn't divorce before their anniversary party. Doris had not been amused.

Daniel had been away more than usual, as well, on business. While they'd grown apart over the years, each with their own interests, Vivian found herself missing him. She'd been having trouble sleeping, as she suspected her grandfather had, and had been having dreams that left her feeling uneasy. Most of them involved water, being in it or near it or on it, dark water that swirled beneath or around her, threatening to drown her – and three times now, she awakened gasping for air, feeling as if a great weight were pressing down on her chest. And even more disturbing to Vivian, a few times in the house and on the grounds, she'd thought she'd seen – shadows, as if someone was lurking who didn't want to be seen. It had happened twice at the foot of the stairs, in the upstairs hall near the doorway to the now unused third floor, and once as she was leaving the garden.

At first Vivian's thoughts had gone to the practical – perhaps she was just tired or needed an eye exam or visit to her doctor. She'd wanted to talk to Glenn about it – he'd always been the one she could go to for comfort, but he'd been looking so worn out, she didn't want to worry him – and speaking with Doris had been out of the question. She could just imagine what her grandmother would say to her, the looks she'd give Vivian. So, Vivian had kept her concerns to herself.

She let out a sigh and regarded her grandmother. Was it Vivian's imagination, or did she look a bit pale? Perhaps, despite her cold manner, she was more worried about her husband than she let on? "I'm sure he'll be home soon," Vivian said.

"He had better," Doris replied, downing the remainder of her sherry.

18

Nora and Kat sat across from one another, perched on tall stools, at the long, stainless steel work counter in the center of The Pepper Pot's huge kitchen. Between them handwritten menus, calendars and notes were strewn about. There was a pile of cookbooks at Nora's elbow, and she had pushed her black-framed cat-eye glasses on top of her head, holding back her unruly curls. She was peering intently into a worn copy of Julia Child's Mastering the Art of French Cooking, one of her favorites.

"Those glasses would probably do you more good on your face than on top of your head," Kat said, grinning.

"You sound like Bernie," Nora replied.

"I could think of worse folks to emulate," Kat quipped back. Bernie Pepper and her older sister were two of Kat's favorite people, and they returned the feeling practically adopting Nora's best girlfriend as their honorary granddaughter.

Nora and Kat were in the middle of their regular Sunday afternoon planning meeting for the coming week, figuring out what supplies and fresh foods they would need, how much help, who would do what and when. Over the past few years, the two women had become a well-oiled machine, and while Kat would say she worked for Nora if asked, Nora considered her a partner in The Pepper Pot. Beside each woman there was a large mug of coffee, Kat's laced with loads of cream and sugar, Nora's with whole milk. There were two forks lying in the remains of the left over triple chocolate cake that was their breakfast. Kat had a smudge of chocolate on the corner of her lip, and Nora looked up and grinned at her, pointing to her own lip. Kat smirked and wiped at her mouth with a nearby napkin.

"So what do you think about doing the bouillabaisse for Harvey and Donald's soup course?" Nora asked, turning the cookbook toward her friend.

"More fish?" Kat said. "We weren't very lucky with that at the Waldemar's."

Nora sighed. "Let's just put that behind us, okay?" she said uncomfortably. "I can start the stock for this on-"

"Nora," Kat interrupted. "Really. What do you think was going on? Was that freaky or what?"

"- on Wednesday afternoon," Nora continued, trying to ignore her friend. She definitely didn't want to think about that night – nor about Bernie's old photo album and what that might mean and her visions of the little girls and –

"What does your grandmother say?" Kat asked conspiratorially, leaning forward on her elbows, her coffee mug cradled in her hands. She took a drink, peering at Nora over the rim.

"What makes you think I talked to Bernie about it?" Nora asked.

Kat looked at her, dumbfounded. "Well, why wouldn't you?"

Nora shook her head and turned back to the cookbook, avoiding Kat's gaze.

"Mister Waldemar saw something," Kat said. "I could see it on his face." She reached over and nudged Nora on the elbow. "And you saw something, too, I know you did." Nora looked up suddenly. "What was it?" Kat asked.

"Nothing!" Nora said, "Can't we just get back to-"

The phone rang, startling both women. Kat reached for it. "This conversation is just beginning," she said as she picked up the phone. Nora scowled at Kat. "Pepper Pot, this is Kat!"

Nora watched as Kat crinkled her eyebrows and looked pointedly back at her. "Sure," she said. "We were just talking about you." She held the phone out toward Nora. "It's Bernie," she said. "She says it's important."

19

Glenn Waldemar lay back on his pillow, panting, his heart thudding in his chest. It was the dream again. Them. Calling to him. Crying. Screaming. Reaching. Wanting him to... He looked around the darkened room, lit by the glow of the monitor attached to his body by several thin cords. The sound had been turned off so as not to disturb him, and the room and halls were just as quiet, if not more so, than his own bedroom at home. He adjusted his sight, blinking several times, and saw that he was alone and that he was all right. The nightmare he'd just experienced was receding but it was certainly not forgotten. He looked up at the monitors, the white, green and red lights blinking steadily. All must be well, he thought, otherwise one of the very attentive nurses who worked the night shift would have rushed in. He laid his hand flat on his chest, feeling his steady heartbeat. *Just a dream*, he said to himself, taking a deep breath and blowing it out slowly, just like his physical therapist had shown him. *Slow and easy.... Slow and easy....*

He reached up and wiped at his eyes. If Doris had been there, she'd have admonished him for his emotion, but he couldn't help it. Why, he thought, after all this time, was he being plagued with this? After all these years? Why couldn't the past just – remain in the past? And there was no one, no one he could talk to about it. Except Doris. He could never.... Could he? What would happen if he did? Finally, told someone?

Under his blanket, he clenched and unclenched his hands. He was so cold. He had been since – that night. Seeing the little girls, the massive, old clock – had been shocking. Especially since he knew very well the clock was no longer there, in its old spot in the hall, standing sentinel as it had for nearly eighty years before....

No, he thought to himself, he had to put it all out of his mind. Hadn't he, after all, nearly accomplished that? There had been a time when that was all he could think about, but Doris had set him straight, hadn't she? Thank God for Doris and her steel backbone, her sights on the future. Because of her, he'd survived, hadn't he? Secrets and loss and pain – until now.

Out in the hall, he saw the shadow of one of the nurses passing by. It was comforting knowing they were out there, awake, watching, making sure he was safe. Day or night, they were just moments away should anything happen, or should he feel alone, frightened – not like it was at home, a myriad of rooms, finely appointed, yes, but empty. That big, old house with no one in it except himself, Doris, Vivian and Daniel, when he was in town for business.

He wondered for a moment why Vivian and Daniel hadn't had children or if they were planning to – the biological clock was ticking, wasn't that what people said? Vivian was thirty-three, and he supposed she had time yet. Maybe she didn't want children, or maybe Daniel didn't. He'd wanted to talk to her about it, but he sensed it was something she didn't want to talk about, and he was usually pretty spot on about his granddaughter. In fact, he'd never heard her speak about the possibility of having children someday, even when she was a little girl. She hadn't been one to play with dolls, either, even though he and Doris had provided her with them, and every other toy a little girl could possibly want. She preferred to play make-believe, dressing up and pretending to be a queen, a mermaid, a fairy, and when she grew older, it was all hair and clothes and make-up – becoming popular. A good student, though, he and Doris had been sure of that.

Thinking about Vivian made Glenn think about Bettie – poor Bettie. She'd been a beautiful girl, sweet and funny, too, if not particularly bright. He smiled wryly to himself. Perhaps she would have been a good match for him. A better match than Doris if only... She'd had a good heart, though, and Glenn was ashamed at how he'd treated her, how he'd let himself be influenced. How had he been so weak? Allowed the wrong things to be important to him? And he knew now, the dreams wouldn't stop, nor the fear, until he told the truth.

The truth. He pushed the button on the side of the bed, raising himself to a sitting position, and looked out the window at the moonlit grounds beyond. The spring evening seemed so beautiful and still. Yes, he decided, it's time – and what was that quote he'd learned in college? From the tragedy play – Brittanicus, wasn't it? By Jean Baptiste Racine? Yes, he thought, that was it. *There are no secrets that time does not reveal.* Yes, it was time, he thought, to talk about what had happened so many years ago. But it was only right that he spoke to Doris first. After all, she had as much to lose – if not more – than he did.

20

Nora rolled down the front windows of the Jeep and let the warm, spring air catch in her hair as she drove. Next to her, Kat tapped her foot in time to the music that was wafting softly from the radio, her purple sunglasses perched on her pert nose. Her short, bright red hair glinted in the sun, and played on the freckles sprinkled generously across her nose – freckles that Nora knew most men who saw Kat Kalinowski thought were absolutely adorable. Kat called them her 'secret weapon' for dating. Bernie had been insistent on the telephone that Nora should bring Kat along and that they should come to the cottage at exactly nine p.m. sharp. She glanced at the clock on her dash – 8:52. She was right on time. Dusk had just fallen, casting long shadows in the piney woods.

Nora turned onto the dirt lane that wound past the barn studio and into the woods toward the cottage. As she approached, she grimaced when she saw the little, white truck parked in the drive emblazoned with the logo SPECTRAL INVESTIGATIONS on the side along with a misty looking ghost that resembled the figure in Edvard Munch's painting The Scream. Nora shook her head. "Damnit," she said under her breath.

"What?" Kat said opening her door and putting a booted foot on the dirt drive. "I think he's kind of cute."

"Stewart Schmidt?" Nora said. "Really?"

Even in the dimness, Nora could see Kat's cheeks pink up. "Well," she said hesitantly. "Yeah. Kind of, I mean."

"I thought you said he was a –"

"I might have been, you know, kind of wrong about him," Kat said. She was blushing furiously, piquing Nora's curiosity, but they didn't have time to get into that right now.

"Uh-huh, right," Nora said. "We will definitely be talking about that later." Kat just shrugged noncommittally.

The front screen door banged and Bernie emerged from the cottage, her green, plaid flannel shirt flapping as she strode toward

Nora. She held up a hand. "Now, before you say anything – " Bernie started.

"Bernie – I told you I – "

"I know, I know," Bernie said. She patted Nora's arm as she reached her and then began to walk alongside her toward the door. "Just give Stewart a chance. He – helps us sometimes. With all those doo-hickies he has. I know you think it's a buncha bull crap but –"

"It's pretty cool, actually," Kat chimed in.

"Thanks for your assistance," Nora said wryly.

Kat grinned. "Anytime."

"I'm only doing this for you," Nora said to her grandmother. "And Bobbi."

Bernie's eyes misted a little behind her silver-framed spectacles. "We love you, too," she said, giving Nora's hand a squeeze. Nora squeezed back. She probably loved this woman more than anyone in the world – but she hadn't been completely honest. Truth be told, she was curious as well, especially after finding the photograph of the Pepper sisters and realizing how much they looked like the mysterious twin girls who'd been appearing to Nora. What did that mean? Was it just some – spirit – trying to get her attention by… Holy crap, she thought, now I sound just like Bernie and Bobbi! She shook it off and followed the other women up the little stone path.

Inside the cottage, to her chagrin, the big, round oak table in the large, open kitchen and dining area looked to be set up for one of Bobbi or Bernie's "readings". Nora hadn't known exactly what to expect – but not this. They'd gone all out, placing the lace table cloth Great

Great-Grandma Eulie Pepper had crocheted upon it, its beautiful swirls and scallops hanging over the sides of the worn, waxed wood. That table cloth only got used for special occasions. That Bernie and Bobbi saw this gathering as a "special occasion" heightened Nora's anxiety more than a little.

There was also one of Bernie's special ceramic bowls in the center of the table, the ones she made of black clay that she'd had imported from somewhere in Brazil. It had been placed in the center of the table filled with water. Rain water, Nora was betting, from the large, wooden barrels that sat on the north side of the barn. They always used it when doing any of their "workings", as they called them. This bowl had a white spiral glazed into the inside bottom, and that spiral seemed to glow against the black clay, making it appear to float on the surface of the water. A wreath of herbs and flowers surrounded the bowl, cradling it like a green nest. Candles were lit, as well, white and blue ones, and near the table Stewart stood with his back to them, arms akimbo, while Bobbi waved a feather over a burning bowl of sage and cedar, the smoke wafting over his shoulders. She turned to Nora.

"Smudge, dear?" she smiled sweetly.

"Do I have to?" Nora asked, knowing the answer.

"Hell, yes, you have to," Kat said, nudging her forward. "Cleanse away the negativity, right?"

"Yes, dear," Bobbi said, shooting her a grin. Nora raised an eyebrow at Kat. *Thanks a lot.* Kat shrugged back at her. *No problem.*

Bobbi handed the bowl and feather to Stewart. "He'll do you – and Katherine." She patted Stewart, who glanced at Nora nervously, on the shoulder. "He's learning," she said. "Aren't you, dear? Do be gentle on him."

Stewart nodded, and Nora walked resolutely toward him, throwing her arms out. She knew the drill. How many times had her grandmother and great-aunt required it – and Nora remembered rushing into the tub as soon as she returned home from the cottage so her mother wouldn't smell the cedar smoke on her and start one her tirades. Stewart bent and started at her feet, as Bobbi instructed him, waving the feather over the smoking bowl as he rose with the smoke toward Nora's head. She breathed in a deep breath, and she had to admit, the acrid smelling smoke was comforting, reminding her of her childhood and the happy times she'd spent in this home with her grandmother. She turned and let Stewart smudge her back. When he tapped her on the shoulder with the feather, just like Bernie used to do, Nora sat at the round table. Kat stepped up, and Nora was amused to see that both she and Stewart blushed slightly.

When he'd finished, Stewart placed the bowl on the table at Bobbi's elbow. "Okay if I get things turned on now?" he asked, looking at the two older women.

"Good idea," Bernie said. "We'll just get settled."

Nora watched as Stewart sat in his place at the table. At his right, on a small, separate folding table were a number of gadgets, which he was busily turning on, and checking cord and cable connections. "What is all that stuff?" Nora asked.

"These are just some of the tools I use," he said, perking up at the question. "To gauge any paranormal activity."

"Like on those ghost hunter shows on television?" she asked, raising an eyebrow.

"Well, most of those are embellished," he said, turning on a small monitor screen. "You see, they –"

"Right," Nora snorted. "And what you do is some how different? Or better? Or more *accurate*?"

Kat reached over and gave her a light swat on the arm. "Give him a chance!" she said, nodding at Stewart who smiled shyly.

"Yes, Nora, please," Aunt Bobbi joined in.

"Okay, okay," Nora said, raising her hands in surrender.

Behind them Bernie stopped her puttering in the kitchen and brought a tray over to the table. On it were five Blue Willow china cups filled with a light-colored, fragrant liquid. "Here," she said. "Everyone have one of these." She began passing the cups around the table. Nora held hers to her nose and breathed in the steamy fragrance.

"Is that ginger?" she asked.

"Ginger, jasmine and a bit of mugwort," Bernie answered.

"Helps boost our – abilities," Bobbi added.

"I don't need mine boosted, thank you very much," Nora said. "But it's yummy."

"We should serve this at the next Ladies' Tea at the Garden Club," Kat said.

"Right," Nora replied. "That's all we need. Psychic gardeners."

"I could think of worse things," Bernie gruffed.

"Let's get started," Bobbi interrupted. Nora and Bernie sighed at the same time. "Are you ready, Stewart?"

"Yes, m'am," he replied.

"Just Bobbie, dear," she said. "That will do."

"Yes, m- I mean, Bobbi," he said.

Bobbi looked over at Bernie, who was arranging a cushion on her chair. She was thin as a rail and the wooden chairs hurt her "tookus" as she called it. "You'll take the lead tonight, sister, is that right?"

"Sure," Bernie replied, sitting down. She took a deep drink of her tea.

"This is so exciting!" Kat said.

"Shhhhhh!" said Bobbi.

"Sorry," Kat replied sheepishly.

Bernie took a deep breath. "Let's all drink together," she said, nodding at the others. They all picked up their cups and drank, then placed their respective cups on the table before them. Bernie reached out her hands, gesturing to the others. Bobbi took her right hand and Nora her left. Nora reached her right hand out to Kat who did not look one bit disappointed that she would be holding hands with Stewart. Who'd have thunk it? Nora smiling to herself. She made a mental note to quiz her best friend about her unexpected crush when they were alone. From the looks of things, she thought, that little crush went both ways, too.

Bernie took a couple of deep breaths, and Bobbi followed suit, both sisters' eyes closed. Nora tried to concentrate, but she felt a bit silly even though she was familiar with her grandmother's and great aunt's ways. She kept imagining how they must look, sitting there together, holding hands, the great bowl of water and lit candles between them. It helped not a little that she'd mentioned the hokey ghost hunter shows a few moments before. They must look exactly like those nuts on television, she thought. But more than her own silly feelings, she loved her grandmother and aunt – and when Bernie had called her, an uncharacteristic hitch in her throat, Nora could not refuse her. So, she decided, she would participate and keep her doubts to herself.

Bernie let out a deep breath and released their hands. The room was dim, the candlelight dancing on the walls and ceiling. "Our goal tonight," Bernie began, "Is to try to contact our sister, Elizabeth Louise Pepper. Our Bettie."

21

At age eighty-two, Doris Waldemar was proud of the fact that she was still able to drive herself around, though she disliked being rushed as she was this afternoon. When Glenn called her, over excited and insistent that she come to his bedside immediately, her intuition told her she needed to get to Valley-Green Memorial as soon as possible. There was a sense of foreboding in her stomach that she disliked, a sense of powerlessness, that some wheel was turning – a wheel her hands were not directing. She'd dressed hurriedly, but impeccably, changing from the silk caftan she'd been wearing as she relaxed in the library to a tailored pale salmon-colored suit and matching shoes. She was a board member at Valley-Green Memorial, after all, and she needed to look like one at all times when she was on the premises. Not a hair out of place.

Glenn's cardiac specialist, Miranda Kim, was just exiting the building as Doris approached. "Missus Waldemar!" she greeted. "So nice to see you." She held out a hand, which Doris took gingerly in her gloved fingers.

"Doctor Kim," Doris replied. "How is my husband? Have you – spoken to him today?"

"Briefly," Kim said. "This morning." She still hadn't released Doris' hand, which was making the older woman most uncomfortable. She disliked being touched overly much, and could not help her feelings of repulsion when the doctor patted Doris gently on the hand. "You must miss him," Kim said. "It's so sweet to see two people who've been together as long as –"

"When can he come home?" Doris said abruptly, pulling her hand away, resisting the urge to rub it on her skirt.

Kim's smile wavered. "Of course," she said. "As you know, he was well enough to go back home from the hospital – but he was so agitated, and of course, he – and you as well, m'am are always welcome at Valley Gr-"

"Doctor?" Doris said impatiently, tapping her foot.

"As far as I'm concerned," she said. "I can release him whenever he's -"

"Excellent," Doris said. "Please do that immediately."

"But Mister Waldemar said –"

"Immediately, please," Doris said, her mouth a straight line.

"But, I was just – " Kim pointed helplessly toward the parking lot.

"Shouldn't take you too long, should it Doctor Kim?" She fixed her blue eyes on the other woman.

"No," Kim said tightly. "I'll take care of it. Right now."

When Doris walked in Glenn's room, he was sitting up in a chair looking out the window at the beautifully manicured lawn, the dogwood and forsythia in bloom, splashing the incredibly new spring green foliage with pink and yellow flowers. Glenn turned hearing the click of her heels on the linoleum, and she could see at once that he was bursting to talk with her, more excited that he'd been in many, many years. There was a look about his eyes that reminded her of when they were young, and for a moment she was taken aback, remembering how handsome he'd been, how much she'd wanted to be married to him. She shook her head and cleared her throat. She didn't need any of that right now. She crossed the room and sat in the high-backed chair opposite him. "Whatever is the trouble?" she asked. "You were positively demanding on the phone. You know how I hate th-"

"Doris," Glenn said. He leaned over and put his hand on top of hers. "It's time,"

"Time for what?" Doris asked. "Are you talking about coming home?"

"No, dear, I…" He squeezed her thin fingers insistently. "We need to tell – someone - about – about Bettie Pepper. And –"

"Are you insane!" Doris hissed, springing up from the chair. She walked quickly over to the door and closed it quickly when whirled on her husband. "Glenn, you stop it right now! What are you thinking?"

"Sit down, Doris!" Glenn said forcefully, and despite herself, she did, surprised at his impertinence. How dare he speak to her in that manner?

"Glenn," she said, making a concerted effort to change her tone. "You haven't been well, dear, and –"

"Oh, don't try that," he chided. "That concerned wife tone. It's beneath you."

"I *am* concerned!" she insisted. "Very much so!"

"Maybe," the old man said, sticking his chin out stubbornly. "But not about me."

Doris' face flushed. "Well, that's just – "

"Doris," Glenn said, sighing wearily, "We're old. Aren't you tired of – keeping this secret?"

"Do you understand what this will mean?" she asked him. "What could happen?"

"Of course," he said. "Don't you realize how many times I've thought about this? What happened? What –"

Doris sat forward suddenly and put her hand on Glenn's. "So, you're – determined?" she asked him, forcing herself to look into his eyes. She noted the sudden flash of surprise on his face, a look of hope, even.

He swallowed, and then looked into her eyes. His were wet with unshed tears, which disgusted Doris, but she knew it would behoove her to keep that disgust off her face. She managed a smile for him. "Yes," he said quietly. "It's the right thing to do, Doris."

"You know," she said after a moment, patting his bony fingers. "You're right. We are old. And we're not going to last forever, are we, dear? It would be a good thing to go out of this world with a clean slate, wouldn't it."

Glenn sighed audibly with relief. "It would," he said gratefully. "Oh, Doris, you've always looked out for us, haven't you?"

"I have," she said, leaning over and brushing his cheek with a dry kiss. "Of course, I have. My darling."

22

At the round, oak table the candles flickered, making the shadows in the room dance. On the table near Stewart, small monitors glowed in the dimness. Bernie put her hand on her sister's arm. They both had welled up at the mention of Bettie, their gazes locked on one another. In that moment Nora realized that the wound of losing their sister, of never knowing what had happened to her, had never closed for either of them. Not really. "How long has it been?" she asked gently. "I don't remember, exactly, I'm sorry."

"It's all right, dear. Not like we talk about it much – not anymore at least. She's been gone since 1937. So – let's see...seventy-five years? She was just seventeen years old." Bobbi said. "I was thirteen and Bernie was nine."

"Oh, " Kat said. "I'm so sorry. I had no idea. What did she die of?"

Bernie and Bobbi looked at one another. "Well," Bernie said, rubbing her jaw. "We – we don't know, exactly – how or even *if* she's dead. Not for sure. Though that's most likely. Even if she was alive – well, she'd be in her nineties by now."

"What happened?" Kat asked.

"She ran away – or was taken away – or something," Stewart said. Nora threw him a sharp glance. Just how much time had he been spending with Bernie and Bobbi anyhow? Who was he to be jumping in on her family's stories?

Stewart's glance wavered under Nora's glowering gaze. "Well, they – told me about it," he said nervously.

"It's fine, bunny," Bernie said, reverting to Nora's little-girl nickname. "Stewart was interested – and he wanted to help."

"Bernie!" she said, embarrassed at her grandmother's use of her childhood nickname.

87

"Oh, shush," Bernie said. "We're among friends. You know, in its day, Bettie's disappearance was a huge mystery. A – you know – cold case. I'm surprised Lucien didn't ever say anything about it." Nora colored at the mention of Lucien's name and Bernie noted her granddaughter's discomfort with a wry smile. Then she picked up her cup and drained the last of her herbal tea. "Let's get started, shall we?" She reached into her shirt pocket and took out the sepia photograph of the three Pepper sisters and laid it in the center of the table near the bowl and candles.

Bobbi added a light blue hair ribbon. "That was hers," she said. "See, she's wearing it in the photo. Sister, remember Momma made us those matching dresses?" She smiled sweetly.

"I do remember," Bernie said. "Momma was so proud of them." She looked at the others. "All right. Nora and Katherine, I'll need your energy and concentration while Bobbi and I try to reach out to Bettie, all right?"

Kat shook her head, eager to help. But Nora's stomach tightened. Suddenly she was remembering the party again, how she'd felt when she'd seen the twins standing in the hallway and the way it had seemed like all the air had been sucked out of the room and the floor was caving in beneath her. She wasn't keen on the possibility of feeling any of those things again, especially in the presence of Stewart Schmidt and his suspicious equipment. Her hands became cold and clammy, and she wiped them on her pants, looking nervously at the floor. No one seemed to notice her discomfort, however, focused as they were on Bernie.

"Stewart, you do what you do with your thingy-ma-bobs over there and let us know if you detect anything, okay?"

"You've got it," Stewart answered, businesslike, almost chipper. It was apparent he was in hog heaven. He placed a small microphone near the center of the table. "I'll get everything on tape. Well – not tape. You see it's a digital recording system, which means –"

"Thanks! That'll be swell, dear," Bernie interrupted. Stewart clamped his lips together. It was apparently not the time for the technology lecture. Nora snickered, earning her a glare from both Bernie and Kat. She cleared her throat and settled back into her chair.

"All right then," Bernie said, taking a deep breath. She closed her eyes and held her palms up and out. "We are reaching out tonight to our sister, Bettie, be she in this world or beyond. We ask to be surrounded by protective light as we go on our journey this evening, and to be kept from harm, and give thanks for that protection." With that, Bobbi lifted the still smoking dish of sage and cedar and held it over the water bowl in the center of the table, moving it in a circular motion. Nora watched as a spiral of smoke rose and disappeared toward the ceiling. She noted an odd, almost electrical feeling at the edges of her consciousness, as if something had been switched on. She blinked, trying to ignore it.

Bernie reached out then, and Bobbi took her hand nodding to the others who all joined their hands around the table. Bernie took another deep breath, then another. Nora looked toward her grandmother and saw she looked as nervous as Nora felt, which increased her anxiety all the more. "What is it?" she asked.

"I – " Bernie began, and then clamped her lips shut and looked to her sister.

"I feel it, too, sister!" Bobbi said and then turned to Nora. "This isn't something we usually do," she explained. "Reaching out to – well….. You know, we do readings and give advice- not usually – this." She squeezed her sister's hand. "How about if we talk about Bettie a little, sister? Remember her."

"That could work," Bernie said gratefully.

"Remember how sweet she was?" Bobbi said. "She never seemed to have a temper with either of us littler ones."

"She didn't, did she," Bernie said, smiling gently. "Even when Momma made her look after us."

Bernie and Bobbi were looking into one another's eyes, their gazes locked, and it was plain to Nora that some connection had been made between them. The air was charged, and to prove that point, one of the devices at Stewart's elbow suddenly lit with a pale blue light, a zig zag registering across its screen. His head turned toward it like lightening, his eyes squinting at the gauge from behind his glasses. "What's happening?" she whispered to him.

"Shhhhhh!" He threw Nora an impatient glance and leaned over to turn some of the dials on his machines. Nora glowered at him. She looked over at Kat but she had her eyes closed in concentration.

"I don't know if you remember, sister," Bobbi continued. "But for a few months before she disappeared, she'd started going off on her own more than usual."

"Well, she was sixteen," Bernie said. "Of course she would-"

"And she had that spot up in the hay loft –she'd go up there and – just lie there sometimes, daydreaming. Momma was getting frustrated with her. I remember that. It was so unlike Bettie. She was always such a good girl."

"Huh," Bernie huffed. "I don't remember her doing that."

"You were little, still," Bobbi said. "I was older. I remember one time I'd gone out to the barn – I don't know what for and I heard her up there. She was – "

Suddenly, all the candles between them on the table blew out, as if a strong breeze had come in to the room. It was suddenly dark, but for the dim lights on Stewart Schmidt's equipment which blinked, making a soft *zzzzzzzztttt*. There was a crackling in the air around them, like a faint sound of radio static or interference. Nora was aware that the temperature in the room had begun to drop, raising goose bumps on her arms. She looked around the table, but it was hard to discern the faces of the participants in the dark. Then, at her right Stewart squeezed her hand suddenly and hard, crushing her fingers. "Ow!" she cried out, and turned toward him. He was sitting back in his chair, his back straight and stiff, his head thrown back. His eyes were open, and she could see the whites of them, fixed on the center of the table above the bowl of water where a mist had gathered, swirling.

And then she heard it, the soft singing. The voice of a young girl. Faint, whispering. *Every time it rains, it rains pennies from heaven....*

Bernie clutched Nora's hand at her left, both her hands now in a vise. Across the table, Bobbi had started to cry. "Singing," she said. "She was in the loft. Singing."

Don't you know each.... cloud....contains.....

Nora turned to her right and in the dimness could see Stewart, his body stiff and eyes focused staring at the ceiling, his mouth was open and the song seemed to be coming from inside him though his lips were not moving. She gasped, her fingers becoming numb in his death grip. She opened her mouth to speak, but nothing would come out.

....pen....sssss.....frooooom...heav.... The song became intermittent, laced with more static and then stopped completely. Next to her Stewart inhaled sharply, sitting up so suddenly that he upset his teacup, spilling the liquid onto Grandma Eulie's tablecloth. The candles on the table re-ignited, flickering crazily. Bernie and Bobbi were sobbing in earnest, now, and across the table, Kat still sat, seemingly oblivious to everything that was happening. Her eyes were still closed, a gentle, almost beatific smile on her face.

"Kat?" Nora whispered.

The other woman's eyes flew open, then, but they were no longer Kat's blue eyes that stared into her own, they were brown – dark brown flecked with gold, just like Nora's – and Bernie's and Bobbi's. "I want them back," she said in a voice that was not her own, and then slumped sideways in her chair, held up only by the hands that held hers on either side.

23

Lucien Pike sat in Perky's nursing a cup of coffee. He loved the old diner, which served old fashioned, blue place special-type meals, comfort food, like meatloaf and mashed potatoes, goulash and buttermilk fried chicken with sweet potatoes. He loved it here as much for its clientele, however, as he did the food – working cops and ex-cops, the old retired guys who liked to gather and tell stories about present and past cases, some won and some lost, that they'd worked here in Ashton Bay and beyond. Perky's also had the best blueberry pie in town, Lucien's favorite. The best aside from that Nora made at The Pepper Pot – and used to make in their own kitchen.

He'd been thinking about her more than usual lately. The sight of her lying in that ambulance, bleeding and disoriented, had shaken him. She hadn't been seriously hurt or ill since he'd known her – maybe a cold or the flu here or there, like anyone, but essentially she was healthy and strong, and it had been upsetting to see her otherwise, though he doubted she, or anyone else had realized exactly how upset he'd been. Oh, yeah, he thought wryly, he was a cool cat, wasn't he? And wasn't that one of the reasons he and Nora weren't together any longer?

He thought back to that night, riding in the ambulance with his ex-wife. She'd just blacked out again, and in her half daze had said his name and reached out for him. He'd taken her hand, which felt small and cold in his, and he'd had to turn away for a moment, so the paramedic wouldn't notice his emotion. At the hospital, he'd called Bernie, and then faded away when she and her sister arrived. Even though he'd had the courtesy to make the call, Nora's grandmother had still given him the stink-eye. She was still mad at him, and he supposed he couldn't blame her. She'd been so good to him when he and Nora were together, and when they divorced, he was pretty sure she felt he'd divorced her, too.

He felt like a heel. Maybe they should have tried harder, he thought – maybe *he* should have – or at least not been so quick to agree when Nora suggested that maybe it would be better if they were apart. He realized now, though it was another thing regarding Nora and their marriage that he didn't like to admit, especially to himself, that perhaps when she'd made that suggestion what she'd really wanted was for him to fight for her, for them. But he hadn't. He'd just agreed. To Nora it must have looked like he hadn't cared at all about their marriage, about her. He drained his cup and set it down on the table, sighing. Well, it was done now, wasn't it? He and Nora were water under the bridge.

The waitress came by with a fresh pot and he pushed his cup toward her for a refill, giving her half a smile. She blushed a little as she poured. "Can I get you anything else, Detective?" she asked.

"Do you have any blueberry pie?" he asked.

She grinned. "Coming right up," she replied. "Warmed just slightly, right?"

"Yep," he said. "Take the chill off. Thanks." He watched her walk off toward the kitchen. "In the oven not the microwave, please!" he called after her.

The waitress turned on her heel and gave him a grin. "I know, I know," she said.

The front door opened, then, and three of the old guys came in, John Santo, who'd been the lead homicide detective back in the fifties, Dave Crustion whom everyone called Crusty, and Walter Solinski, the oldest of the three at ninety-seven. He'd been a beat cop in Ashton Bay, back in the thirties when Bettie Pepper disappeared. He raised a hand and they returned his greeting, walking over toward him.

"Workin' hard, I see," Crusty said, grinning. "How's that old S.O.B. DeBrun treating you?"

Lucien grinned. "Like the dog I am," he replied, earning him a clap on the shoulder from the old cop.

The waitress arrived at the table with the pie and set it next to his elbow. "Interest you boys in some of this fine blueberry pie?" he asked.

"What's in it for you?" Walter asked, sitting immediately. "Heat mine up and put some ice cream on it," he said to the waitress.

Santo and Crusty looked at one another. "Guess we're having pie," Santo said.

"Guess we are," said Crusty. He waved a finger in a circle over the table. "Coffees, too," he said. "You know how we like 'em."

She nodded. "Two black, one with lots of cream and sugar."

"That's right," Walter said. "The way civilized folks drink it."

"So, what have you got on your mind, son?" Santo asked. "What are you workin'? All that new technology you got downtown now lettin' you down? You need these three big brains here to fill in the gaps?"

Lucien shook his head and chuckled. The waitress dropped off the pie and coffee, and Walter dug in immediately, dripping a bit of melting ice cream on his expertly shaven chin. "Actually, I'm curious," Lucien said. "About an old case. One you probably all remember it, but Walt here may have worked it."

"Ah, stone age then," Crusty said.

"Stuff it down your windpipe, Crust," Walter growled. "And choke on it."

Santo chuckled. "Feelin' the love?" he asked Lucien.

"Indeed," he replied.

Walter wiped at his mouth with his napkin, most of his pie and ice cream already disappeared from the plate. For an old guy, he sure had a good appetite. He took a slurp of his coffee then looked at Lucien. "Must be the Pepper case," he said.

"How do you know that?" Crust asked, tipping his Detroit Tigers cap back on his balding pate.

"Think about it," Walter said. "Who's Pike, here, married to? What case do you think he'd be askin' me about?"

"Was married," Lucien corrected.

Walter rolled his eyes.

"What?" Lucien said.

"Nothin'," Walter said, scraping the last of the blueberries off his plate. "That's your business."

"Right," Lucien said. "So, do you think the case file is still around?"

Walter scratched his head. "Might be," he said. "If so, it's probably pretty sketchy. As I recall, there wasn't much to go on."

"You worked that case, didn't you, Walt?" Crusty asked.

"Some," he said. "I was new on the force. Twenty-three years old, if you can imagine it. That was in '38. She disappeared a few months before, but we were still looking."

"What do you remember?" Lucien asked.

"Like I said," Walt replied. "There wasn't much. She was a nice kid, quiet, pretty. Nice family. Not wealthy, by any means, but they got by okay. The father worked at the machine shop in town, as I remember, and they farmed some. Had three little girls. Nothing out of the ordinary stood out. We asked around the school, too. She had a couple of girlfriends but no one knew anything. One morning her momma went in to wake her up for school and her bed hadn't been slept in. There wasn't anything of consequence missing. She'd just vanished."

"She didn't take any belongings? Nothing?"

"Not that her momma could tell. It was fall, early. September. School had just started back up. And it was dry that year. There weren't any footprints or any other disturbances outside. Like I said, you could hunt up the file, but I don't think there was much in there."

"How about relatives?" Lucien asked. "Family out of town?"

"Yeah, we checked. More than once. There wasn't much family to speak of. You'd find those specifics in the file, I don't remember how many or where they were from – one in

Detroit, I think, but it was all a dead end."

"And the family?"

"The mother, Lila her name was, she never got over it. She got sick and died pretty young, in her forties. Cancer, they said, but you know, losing a child is hard on a body. Especially like that – not knowing what happened. If she was dead or alive. Whether she left on her own or…"

"She didn't run away," Crispy spoke up. He was the second oldest in the group of old timers.

"How you figger?" Walt asked.

"What'd she have to run away from?" Crispy asked. "By all accounts she was a happy kid from a happy family."

Walt leaned forward, his elbows on the table. He looked at the others, a half grin on his wrinkled face. "Well, Crisp, I gotta say I agree with you, " he said. "I said it then, but I was a young fart with no experience – and I'll say it now." He gave Lucien a dark look. "Maybe it wasn't want she was running away *from*. Maybe it was what – or who - she was running *to*."

24

Nora climbed the old, bare oak steps that led to the loft in the barn. Bernie didn't like anyone coming up here, not since Chase died, but Bobbi had invented a shopping list and had agreed to get Nora's grandmother out of the way for a couple of hours so she could look around. It had been two days since they'd met at the cottage to try to contact Bettie, and since then, Nora had been plagued with dreams, her thoughts wandering. She'd been totally useless at The Pepper Pot, and Kat had talked her into a day off since their week was light anyhow.

Kat had no recollection of what had happened to her that evening, nor of the message she'd delivered. Nora hadn't told her about her eyes, the way they'd changed from their usual pretty, bright blue to dark brown. Maybe, she rationalized, that hadn't happened at all. Maybe she'd imagined it. Yes, that had to be what happened, she thought. And if she'd have mentioned it to Kat, well, she'd think Nora had gone bonkers, right? All Kat did remember was a feeling of floating, which she said felt pleasant. She remembered drinking the tea, grasping hands, concentrating on Bernie's voice. But, she'd said, it was as if she'd fallen asleep, not waking until she'd felt Stewart at her side, shaking her shoulder.

Of course, Bernie and Bobbi – and Stewart – had bombarded her with questions. What she had seen, heard, experienced. What I *want them back* meant. Was it a message from Bettie? Or did she mean I *want her back*? Maybe it was their mother, Lila, reaching out, saying she wanted her missing daughter? Stewart wanted to know what she had experienced as well, and as he did so, pointed to this gadget and that one. Nora finally edged him out, pushing in to sit beside Kat and give her a glass of cold water. She'd shot Stewart a look that made him pause and step out of the way. Nora was suspicious of him, of the song that had come out of his mouth – had *he* made that happen? Was it some sort of trick to make his claims as a "paranormal investigator" valid? In any case, she didn't trust him – and she wasn't crazy about him being around her elderly grandmother and aunt – nor her best friend.

When she reached the top of the stairs she paused for a moment and looked around. She used to love coming up here when Papa was alive. She'd adored him, and the feeling was mutual. He would let her lie on her stomach on one of the old, dusty Oriental rugs that covered the wood floor with a cast off piece of canvas or cardboard or paper and paint or draw to her heart's content while he worked on one of his paintings or sculptures. There were still several half-finished canvases propped against the wall, dusty with time. Nora wondered how long it had been since Bernie had come up here herself, or if she'd stopped coming up completely. She wondered if she'd gone through Papa's things, sorted and cleaned, but from the looks of things, nothing had been touched since he'd gotten sick.

One of the only times Nora could remember getting a serious scolding from her grandmother was when she snuck up into the loft one day after another terrible argument with her mother. She had headed to Bernie's on her Vespa. This was before her grandmother had given her Chance's Jeep to drive. She hadn't been planning on going into the loft, but when she got to her grandmother's house, no one was there. She'd wandered into the studio instead, using the key that Bernie kept hidden in an old, rusty watering can on the side of the barn. She remembered how it felt walking in there, like she imagined church felt to some people. The sun was filtering through the high windows, dust dancing in the rays like diamonds and suddenly, she was missing her Papa. She'd loved being around him. He was always entertaining, railing about the government, talking about this artist or poet or philosopher, showing her what he was working on – even the nudes when she was probably too young to see them. His love for her was so –palatable. So blatant. So unlike the way it was for her growing up with Ivy – and a father who was under his wife's thumb.

Nora wandered around the loft, touching her grandfathers brushes, tubes of paint long hardened, jars of turpentine and fixatives and glazes. She didn't know exactly what she was looking for, or why she hadn't been able to get the loft out of her mind since Bobbi had told them about hearing Bettie singing up her and that she'd like to spend time here. She poked about on the shelves and drawers, not wanting to disturb things much – and, she figured, all these things, her grandfather's things, were brought here well after Bettie disappeared.

Against the wall there were several large canvases draped with a discolored linen drop cloth. Nora lifted the corner of the cloth, scaring several large spiders and a slew of dust bunnies out of the fabric. All of the canvases were facing the wall. Nora pulled the cloth completely off, letting it fall to the floor. She tipped one of the canvases back so she could see what was painted on its face.

Nora's breath caught in her throat. On the canvas was a nude painting of Bernie, a young Bernie, but totally recognizable, her now white hair long, dark and curly as Nora's own. She wasn't taken aback because it was a nude, but because it was so incredibly beautiful and unlike her grandfather's other work, which consisted mainly of abstracts and attempts at cubism. It was apparent in every brush stroke that the artist loved his subject very much.

There were six canvases in all. Nora wondered why Bernie kept them up there like that. Perhaps she couldn't bear to look at them, remembering the man who'd painted them and loved her so deeply. As she pulled the last canvas from the wall – a portrait of Bernie this time, a formal one in which she was wearing a white dress cinched at her waist with a pink sash. Behind her a deep, sea green background that accentuated her hair and eyes and blush on her cheeks – Nora realized she was humming. *Every time it rains, it rains pennies from heaven....* There, on one of the wallboards near the floor a small X was scratched into the wood.

Something fluttered in Nora's stomach. She pulled the paintings one by one away from the wall and stacked them carefully on the drop cloth. Then she knelt near the wallboard, tracing the X with her finger. She pushed on the board to no avail, and then looked up to see if it was an indication of anything hidden above. All she saw there were more cobwebs and dust hanging from the rafters.

But when she stood, the floorboard nearest the wall gave a little. Nora dropped back down, pushing on it with her fingertips. She tried pulling it up with her fingers but was unable to get any purchase. On her grandfather's old worktable was a flat paint spatula. She fit the blade under the wood and pulled up a short piece of the floorboard to reveal a hiding place underneath.

Nora's fingers shook as she pulled out the metal tin. It was an old cake tin, probably from a Christmas far past. She'd seen several of them before, around her grandmother's house. She and Bobbi still used them to store odds and ends, like buttons and playing cards and pencils. She sat on the floor, cross-legged and placed her fingers on the edge of the lid, prying it up gently. It opened with a soft screech of metal on metal.

There, lying in the tin was a fat bundle of letters.

25

"I need a favor," Doris Waldemar purred into the telephone. "Actually, it's for Vivian." Doris listened, waiting for Daniel Spruce to answer. She could imagine the tight look on his face. She knew it well. She knew she made Daniel uncomfortable, always had, and she liked it that way. She also knew that he knew who controlled the money in the family, and she believed that while he cared for Vivian a great deal, Daniel cared about the family's assets a great deal as well.

At the other end of the line, he cleared his throat. "Of course," he said. "What is it?"

"Well, you know, Vivian's been so upset since the party, her grandfather and all – stressed out. I was thinking," she paused, looking out the window at the pond. All the grass and foliage around it had gone brown and dry. "Perhaps she's missing you – in fact, I know she is. How about you invite her to spend the rest of the week and the weekend with you in Chicago. What do you think? She can do some shopping – that always cheers her up. Maybe take her for a romantic dinner?"

Doris heard Daniel exhale but didn't know if it was in relief or that he wasn't crazy about the idea of having his wife with him. She wondered, and not for the first time, whether her grandson-in-law was faithful to Vivian or whether he was seeing someone else during his frequent Chicago business trips. "Sure," he said, finally. "Tell her to pack. I'll have my secretary get a flight set up for her and-"

"Oh, no, no, no, dear," Doris said, sweetly. "This needs to be *your* idea. It would mean so much to her. You understand."

"Of course," he said tightly. "I'll phone her this afternoon."

"Now would be a good time," Doris said insistently. "I think she's just getting out of the shower."

"Yes," he said. "Of course it would."

The phone made a sharp click as Daniel hung up. She placed the receiver gently on the telephone cradle and turned as Vivian walked into the room holding a cup of coffee. She regarded Doris at the window. "It's awful, isn't it?" she said.

"The garden? Yes, it is," Doris said.

"I had a thought about it." Vivian sat in a wing chair beside the empty fireplace, crossing her long legs demurely at the ankles.

"Have you?" Doris replied.

"I think I've come up with a solution," Vivian said. "We could dredge the pond and fill it in. Start a new-"

"Absolutely not!" Doris said, more vehemently than she meant to.

Vivian sat up in her chair, a confused look on her face. "But I —"

Doris crossed the room quickly and sat in the chair opposite her granddaughter. "What I mean is," she said, trying to moderate her voice. "I've been thinking about it, too. And – you know how much the pond means to your grandfather—"

"Well," Vivian said hesitantly. "Yes, I suppose so. " Doris knew well that Glenn often took to sitting on the little stone bench that sat near the now dead pampas grass on the west side of the pond. He'd sit there for hours, sometimes, just staring at the water, perhaps watching the fish.

"I was thinking about a Japanese rock garden," Doris said. "You know, kind of – what's the word? Zen. Yes, a Zen garden. Wouldn't that be lovely? And no plants to worry about."

"Well, I —" Vivian began. "Yes. I guess that might be nice. I'd never thought of that." Just then she startled as her cell phone chimed in the pocket of her plush robe. She pulled it out, smiling softly as she looked at the screen. "It's Daniel," she said, pushing a button to answer.

"That's nice, dear," Doris said, rising. "I'll just give you some privacy." She exited the study, a tight, secret smile on her lips.

26

Stewart put on his best headphones, the Bose SoundTrue set, and adjusted some settings on the digital recorder. He wanted to be sure he'd heard what he thought he'd heard, what Bernie and Bobbi had told him they'd heard, coming out of his mouth, no less. After that, he intended to examine the footage he'd gotten on the digital camera. Unfortunately, he'd only set up one camera, and it had been focused away from him, so he wouldn't be able to witness the phenomena the women had told him about. He was at the same time excited – nearly giddy, in fact – and a little scared. He'd been ghost hunting since he was a kid, but he'd never really experienced much more than seeing a few possible orbs in some photographs and recording some very sketchy EVPs. Well, *possible* EVPs.

Stewart knew what people thought of him. Most people, anyhow. That he was a joke, a fake, delusional even. There were people – people like Nora Pepper, he suspected – who thought he was trying to bilk frightened folks out of some money. But the truth was, Stewart didn't charge for what he did, for his investigations. Sometimes if a person was grateful - although it was usually because Stewart's equipment *didn't* pick up anything otherworldly. And if they were grateful, they might make a donation, which he happily accepted. Equipment got expensive, and he liked to give what he did some validity, and money paid for his services proved exactly that, he thought. Especially to people like Nora Pepper – not to mention Stewart's mother, Mary Schmidt, a sensible woman from a good German family who didn't believe in such things as ghosts and hauntings.

There it was, the spot where Bobbi and Bernie Pepper were reminiscing about their missing sister, then a faint crackling is heard, an electrical sound which to Stewart sounds almost like the scratching a phonograph needle makes on a record – and then there it was. The singing. Definitely not his voice, though the Peppers insisted it was coming from his mouth. He thought back and didn't remember blacking out or anything like that. Just sitting at the end of the table, one hand in Nora's and the other in Kat Kalinowski's (that hand had been sweating just a little), monitoring his equipment.

But Stewart not only missed his contribution, but Kat's as well. However, he thought, getting a little giddy, that portion he had on video. He cued it up and sat back viewing it on his computer screen, the room in shadows and the participants glowing in strange colors due to his use of the infrared feature which helped him film better in the darkness. There was Kat, relaxing in her chair, eyes closed. Nora speaks to her and then, there it was – Kat's eyes flying open as she leans toward her friend. "I want them back," she says forcefully, then falls back in her chair, Stewart grasping her hand hard to hold her up. When he stands, he blocks the camera completely, but everything was over by then – or so he thought.

As the video progresses, he sees Kat sitting up in her chair, Nora at her side handing her a glass of water. Bernie and Bobbi are also huddled together, talking earnestly. Then Stewart sees himself walk around the table to turn off the camera and the other equipment. Momentarily he disappears behind it. And then, in the dimness he sees a faint glow standing between the Pepper sisters and Nora, a glow that slowly and faintly takes shape. Stewart leaned forward, his face nearly touching the computer screen. To him it looks like two little girls are standing between the Peppers, starting straight into the camera lens straight at him, holding hands.

27

Glenn Waldemar leaned back on his pile of down pillows and smoothed the blankets down over his thighs. Last nights sleep had been thankfully dreamless, though he'd been anxious about being back in the house for the first time since the fated anniversary party. Doris hired a lovely nurse to ride home with them and help get him settled. He remembered the feeling he'd had, standing on the stoop, the way his heart had beat in his chest and the sheen of sweat that had broken out on his brow. The nurse, Laurie, had asked him if he was all right. She was a petite blonde, and extremely pretty, and Glenn's old habit of wanting to impress a beautiful woman kicked in. He'd smiled, showing his very white teeth and assured her he was fit as a fiddle although he'd felt the total opposite.

As they approached the staircase, his glance had been drawn to the foot of the stairs, the little alcove where the ancient grandfather clock used to stand. In fact, it had been there for so long that there were still four small indentations in the wood floor where its massive, lion-clawed feet used to rest. Doris had placed a small, ornate Restoration Period credenza in its place to hide the marred flooring. She couldn't, however, hide the memories. The sight of the twins had terrified Glenn. It was as if his dreams – or nightmares, depending on how you looked at it – which had come to him more and more frequently over the past few months had materialized. He knew what they wanted, what they had always wanted, and he knew they would not let him rest until they got it or until…he was dead.

Maybe he should have died the night of the party night, he thought. Maybe it was what he deserved. He looked out the window. The bright, spring sun was shining. It was so cheerful, and it should have heartened him – but all he could feel was regret. What had he to show for his life, really? He thought back to the young man he'd been, handsome, born into privilege. He'd been able to go away to the best schools – away from the working class and farming community of Ashton Bay. He'd gotten a business degree – barely, he thought. He'd been a lazy youth, and had to admit had been allowed by his family to be a fairly lazy man. He hadn't had to worry about acquiring a job as one was provided for him in the Waldemar family's shipping business. That had been one of the "perks" of marrying well, as his mother had required of him. Of doing as he was told.

Doris had been a beauty in her day, and from a good family to boot. Her father had been a partner of his father's in their New York offices, and both families had hoped, when he and Doris were only young children, that a match would be made. For Glenn's mother, Eliza, however, it was more than a hope. She made sure it happened. With considerable assistance from Doris who could not have been more like Eliza Waldemar if she had been her very own daughter.

Glenn reached for the cup of tea that was waiting for him on his bedside table. He sipped at it. It was laced with buckwheat honey, just the way he liked. Ah, Doris, he thought. She could be a hard woman. But sometimes – like now – she could be considerate of him, of what he wanted or needed. He was still surprised about her compliance on this matter, however. He'd thought he would have to fight her on it, or perhaps, just do what he needed to do regardless of her own opinions and feelings on the matter. But she'd come around and for a change, allowed him a decision. It was, after all, the right thing to do.

They'd decided on a course of action together, which had made Glenn feel tender toward his wife. There hadn't been a lot of tenderness over the years, and perhaps, now in their old age they could experience a bit of that, no matter what the consequences of what he knew they must do. Much of their marriage had always felt like a business arrangement – indeed, Glenn thought, it was just that if you were to look at it realistically. His true joy had been his daughter, lost too soon, and then his granddaughter, his pretty, smart, lively Vivian.

They'd decided to tell her first. She was their only family, after all, and it was only right to bring her in to the loop so she would not be blindsided when they did what they had to do to make things right. He knew Vivian would be hurt, and that pained him. He only hoped she wouldn't hate him. That would kill him for sure, he thought.

He watched as a group of robins flew past his window, chirping and diving, most likely in search of some fat bugs or worms in the moist, spring grass below. As soon as Vivian was back from her trip to Chicago, he thought. Just a few more days. Then the wheel would be put in motion. Glenn breathed a sigh of relief and lay back on his pillows and closed his eyes.

28

Lucien was getting frustrated and irritable. He disliked going on wild goose chases, and this seemed to be exactly what this was turning out to be. The basement of city hall was cavernous, ancient and acrid, and the moldy air was playing havoc with his sinuses and giving him a pounding headache. Not to mention the lighting down here in the Records Storage Department left a lot to be desired. Added to this, several of the numbered notations of the file boxes had faded making it extremely difficult for him to find the folder he was looking for. What was he expecting, anyway, he thought to himself. The damn file was over seventy years old.

The drafty room echoed suddenly with the sound of the Spanish guitar. The song was *Have You Ever Really Loved a Woman*. It had been their song, his and Nora's. They'd both set it as the ring and text message tone on their cell phones Corny, he knew, but they'd been that he supposed. In love and silly. He'd never bothered to change his. He kept telling himself he'd do it, but he never had. He pulled the phone out of his pocket and checked the message.

-NORA: need to talk to you. Have something to show you. Can we meet ASAP?

Lucien thought for a moment. He regarded the dusty shelves once again and then sighed when he saw that the box he'd been looking for was right there in front of him. He pulled it down and set it on the floor, then turned back to his phone.

-LUC: I may have something to show you 2. Soon. I'll msg you.

-NORA: OK. Don't wait too long. Plz.

-LUC: OK

Lucien picked up the box. The top was crusty with dust. He opened it, thumbing through the few files inside it until he came to the one he'd been searching for. Case number 1938-213P. It was, as Walter Solinski had surmised, disappointingly thin. He left the box open on the table and walked the long aisle to the Xerox and began copying the few pages of notes and photographs. He tucked them into the fresh folder he'd brought with him, replaced the originals and headed out of the gloomy basement. He'd read it over in his office, he decided, see if there was anything helpful in it, and then get back with Nora.

Once in the office, however, he found that all hell had broken loose. A bar fight in the city's South End had produced two stabbing victims, one dead and one in the emergency room at Ashton Bay Medical Center. He threw the Elizabeth Pepper missing person file on his desk and headed out to investigate the crime scene.

29

Nora paced the long living room in the loft apartment she lived in over The Pepper Pot. She'd loved the space for this very room, which took up the length of the apartment on one side and opened into a small kitchen and dining area. Down a short hall off the kitchen was a sizable bedroom and en suite bath. The living room was her favorite room, however, though most people would have been surprised at that, knowing how much Nora loved cooking. But this room faced west and the back of the property which butted up to a thick stand of birch trees. In the evenings, whatever the season, Nora liked to watch the red sun sink down behind those trees, making their papery white bark glow as if they were on fire.

She glanced at her cell phone, which was lying next to the packet of letters on the low, kidney-shaped coffee table, its screen dark. It had been hours since she'd messaged Lucien and she was getting anxious and irritated. What could be going on in a quiet town like Ashton Bay to hold him up for this long? He could have at least had the courtesy to shoot her a short message. She sat down on the sofa in a huff, running her hands through her long hair then letting it fall in curly waves around her face. The newly white strand hung down in her face, a reminder of her frightening evening at the Waldemars' and all that had happened since. She impatiently pushed it back behind her ear so she wouldn't have to look at it.

She ran her finger over the top envelope. It had gone dusky with age, its edges brittle. It was obvious in the weight and texture of the envelopes and paper that it had once been expensive. It was evident in the weight and texture of them. They were love letters, seventeen in all, overly flowery and almost laughably romantic, but Nora imagined that back then, in the 1930s, that was the way the language of love played out. Each letter was signed at the bottom with a formal, scrolling -**G**. And if Nora was right about who'd written them – well, that would open up a whole new mystery about what had really happened to her Great-Aunt Bettie.

Nora looked at her watch. She'd been waiting to hear from Lucien for hours. She sat up impatiently and picked up her cell phone, scrolling uselessly through her incoming texts and calls. Still nothing from Lucien. Leave it to him to forget she wanted – needed – to talk to him! To put her on the back burner like he always seemed to do! Well, that's it, she thought to herself and knew exactly what she was going to do. She'd find out once and for all on her own if she was right about the author of Bettie Pepper's love letters. She picked up the bundle and stuffed it into her bag, threw on a hooded sweatshirt against the evening chill, and headed down to her Jeep.

30

Bernie Pepper was feeling surly and taking it out on a lump of red clay in the studio. Usually, pounding and kneading the stuff helped her center herself and think rationally, but today that just wasn't working. She was worried, about her sister and her granddaughter. Since the evening of Bettie's contact – and Bernie believed that they had indeed contacted her long, lost sister – Bobbi had been withdrawn and quiet, totally unlike her cheerful self. And she seemed to have lost her appetite, which worried Bernie more than a little. Nora had withdrawn as well, but physically, not stopping by the way she usually did. Nor was she returning Bernie's calls. She'd tried to get her granddaughter several times on the phone to no avail.

Bernie was sure that what had happened that night had frightened Nora – and possibly that she'd experienced something she wasn't talking about, something she needed help processing. And Bernie was hurt and frustrated that Nora was not letting her in. Not letting her help.

Something was going on. Bernie knew it. Something that they had put in motion that night – in part, in any case. That was her feeling. They'd added energy to something that she guessed had begun long before that night. She'd tried consulting the cards to get some clarity on exactly what, but everything had felt muddled and dark. As if she were being kept out purposely by something or someone. Was she being blocked purposefully? Or perhaps protected? She disliked not knowing. It made her feel jumpy, anxious – and a little angry.

Her heart was heavy as well, for she now felt she knew for sure the fate of her oldest sister. She was dead. Bernie thought, perhaps, long dead. She knew it was silly, maybe, but since that night, she felt newly grieved. And Bobbi felt it as well. Bernie was sure that was the reason for her sister's malaise, even though they hadn't talked about it. Just that fact concerned Bernie as well. She and Bobbi talked about every little thing – that they hadn't spoken about it since that night – even though Bernie had broached it a few times, Bobbi had shut her down. In fact, she thought, as far as Bernie knew it seemed that no one involved with what had happened that night had spoken about it, and she had to wonder what that meant.

Nora was another matter. She was just plain being stubborn and ignoring Bernie. It was because she was opening up, and Bernie knew that frightened her. If she only knew what Bernie and Bobbi had suspected for such a long time – that Nora's gifts were so much stronger than their own, and that they could be used to help her, to help others. She knew Nora's mother had much to do with that. Ivy had always had distain for her and Bobbi. They'd never had a good feeling about her, but Charlie had loved her to distraction. At nineteen, Ivy had been a beautiful girl, and smart as well. Shy, trusting Charlie hadn't had a chance when she'd set her sights on him. But Ivy had sucked the light out of her boy. Bernie smashed her small, bony fist, stronger than anyone would have believed, down onto the red clay, flattening it. Growing up on the Pepper property, Charlie had been a creature of the woods, building forts, learning the names of plants and birds and insects. A magical boy, sweet and trusting. And Ivy had destroyed that trust, and destroyed Charlie in the end, too.

Oh, she knew well that he'd died in an accident. Accident, indeed! Not that she thought her son had crashed the car on purpose, but hadn't her dreams been haunted by his last moments? In them she was beside him in the car, a silent, ghostly passenger who was helpless to do anything but watch it all unfold. To see exactly what had happened to him, beginning with his arriving at his job at the library that morning and realizing he'd forgotten the one-day reference books he'd borrowed the day before. He knew where he'd left them, lying in a short stack on his bedside table. Three books on the Ojibwe clans that had inhabited the area around Ashton Bay. His he and his son-in-law had gotten into a discussion about it, Lucien mentioning his ancestry and relatives that still lived on Native land on the western side of the state. It had piqued Charlie's interest and he'd wanted to learn more. However, like any librarian, late books irked him even though as a library employee he had more leeway on that than most. He'd turned around and returned home where an unexpected car was parked in his driveway, a dark blue Lincoln Town Car that seemed a bit familiar, though Charlie couldn't place exactly where he'd seen it before.

Inside the house had been both quiet and full. Bernie's experience of it, gliding along at his shoulder in her dreams, was that of an impending storm. Charlie had felt it, too, the heavy hush. Any other time, he'd have called out to Ivy when he entered the back door, but that day, something had stopped him, a cold feeling in his stomach, and he'd mounted the stairs walking softly, both wanting and not wanting to find out what waited for him.

When he'd pushed the bedroom door open, the first thing he'd seen was the stack of library books lying on the bedside table in their neat stack where he'd left them. The second thing he'd seen was Ivy's lover lying on his side of the bed. His wife was on top of him, the curve of her naked back and buttocks reminding him of the shape of a cello, which he'd attempted to play in high school but had never been very good at. The door squealed a little when he pushed it open and he'd thought, incongruously, how many times he'd meant to fix that. Ivy's head turned slowly, her mink-like hair lying across one shoulder. Her face was flushed with love making, but she didn't even look surprised to see him, not startled or upset – or sorry. And while Charlie knew their marriage had not been the happiest one he hadn't expected this He loved Ivy and he was blindsided by her betrayal.

Books forgotten, he'd gotten behind the wheel, blinded by the thrashing in his chest, anger, fear, sadness...spirit Bernie had felt how tightly he was clutching the wheel, could hear the NPR news program he always listened to when he drove that drone on, could feel the sting of hot tears in her son's eyes, his disbelief and confusion, his foot pressing harder and harder on the accelerator, the car straining forward – and panic as he took the wrong turn south into the northbound lane of the highway, directly into the path of oncoming traffic. He was killed instantly. Bernie experienced a sudden bright flash and then nothing and then floating. Floating away, her Charlie, her baby, her son....

She wiped at a tear that had slipped onto her cheek, making a smudge of red clay like war paint on her finely wrinkled skin. There were people in the world, she thought, who were destroyers, and Ivy Barrette was one of them. She'd destroyed Charlie, sucked the joy right out of him – and she'd made Nora feel so ashamed about the gifts she'd been given, ashamed and frightened – that the girl did anything she could to run away from that part of herself. Bernie pushed the clay into a ball and wrapped it in a damp cloth then placed it into a covered plastic container. Eventually, she thought, Nora was going to have to deal with who – and what – she was. And Bernie hoped it would be sooner rather than later.

31

Doris Waldemar may have been old, but she kept in shape. She'd been a member of the Ashton Bay Country Club since marrying into the Waldemar family in 1938. It wasn't as grand as the club she and her family had belonged to back in New York, but for a small community, it was considerably impressive, made more so by the generous donations she'd forwarded it over the years. Doris had always been active, and at eighty-two still swam every day and played a bit of tennis when she could find a partner. One of the young studs that worked as a trainer in the club's gymnasium had shown her how to use some of the weight machines as well, and she especially liked the leg press. She couldn't move a lot of weight but for her age she did very well, pushing seventy pounds of iron weights back and forth with her sinewy limbs. Vivian and Glenn didn't know about these workouts and weren't particularly aware of her strength, and Doris made a point of not drawing attention to it. After all, it was to her advantage to act the little old woman most people expected her to be. She liked being thought of as a bit frail. People did things for her, and that was how she liked it. She was pretty sure her granddaughter and her husband thought she met women friends at the club for cocktails and mahjong, which she did do, just not all that often.

She looked out the kitchen window as she waited for the water to boil and stared at the ruined pond. How she hated it. Always had. It was deep and dark, its bottom rife with greenish black fronds and plants that waved in the water like so many ghostly fingers. Doris remembered when it had been full of green leopard frogs and clever silver fish and water lilies. The dragonflies that dove and swirled above its glassy surface. It had been the jewel of the gardens.

On the stove near her the teakettle whistled. She'd given the part time housekeeper they used the week off. With Vivian gone she and Glenn had the house to themselves. *Isn't it romantic?* she thought bitterly to herself. She steeped the tea for a moment, then added the dark buckwheat honey to the cup and stirred the amber colored liquid. Then from the pocket of her cardigan she extracted the capsules. There were three types, all of which she'd found in the combined medicine cabinets in the house. She smiled to herself. The Internet was a wonderful thing, she thought as she held each capsule one over the cup and then carefully pulled the clear gelatin covers apart. She poured the granules they contained into the tea then stirred again, checking the cup to be sure the drugs had dissolved completely. She placed the cup on a tray with a small plate of butter cookies and headed for the stairs.

She paused on the landing and set the tray carefully on the floor. Below the huge, arched window at the landing was built in mahogany bookshelf that housed several heavy antique volumes. Mostly drivel about land title deeds and such. They'd been old Mister Waldemar's books, Glenn's grandfather, and he'd insisted on keeping and displaying them. Dust catchers as far as Doris was concerned, though she had to admit now that they would be useful. She chose three of the fattest volumes and set them on the edge of the first set of stairs. At the top of the second tier of stairs she quietly lowered herself down and sat on the second step. From her pocket she removed the length of wire she'd gotten from the workbench in the basement. She attached it to the banisters on either side of the steps at the head of the stairs about six inches from the floor pulling it taut and twisting the ends of the wire so it would hold. Then she went back to the landing and picked up the tray and carried it up the remaining flight of stairs, stepping carefully over the wire she installed.

When she pushed Glenn's bedroom door open he was sitting up in bed against his pillows. He'd gotten some of his color back, and Doris had to admit, he was still quite a handsome man for his age. It was too bad he was such a weak man as well. Always had been, for the most part. Of course, she had seen it at the beginning, and even Glenn's mother has spoken with her about it. Said Glenn needed a strong woman like Doris – a woman like she herself was – to steer him through his life. And financially, well, it hadn't been a difficult decision. The combined wealth of the families….and back then, it still wasn't out of the norm to arrange marriages. She and Glenn had been pushed toward one another since she was eight and he was ten years old – at least that's when she became aware of it.

She'd always known she would be Missus Glenn Waldemar. She'd know it practically all her life. And, she knew, so had he. There had been no question regarding who each of them would marry. That's why she and Eliza Waldemar had been so shocked and angered when they found out about trashy, little Bettie Pepper. What in the world had Glenn been thinking?

He smiled at her wanly when she came in the room with the tray. "You shouldn't have carried that, dearest," he said to her. "That's why we have Susan."

"I've sent her home for a few days," Doris replied. "It's just you and I." She set the tray down and handed him the tea. "I thought it would be nice, being alone together. After all, we don't know what will happen...after." She lowered her eyelashes.

Glenn reached out and took her hand. "I know you must be – apprehensive, Doris. Even frightened. I am, too, to be honest. But more about telling Vivian than anything else. Do you think she will hate us?"

Doris looked up at Glenn with just the right amount of tears shining in her blue eyes. "Of course not," she said. "She loves us. And we're all she really has anymore. Except Daniel and –"

Glenn smiled a bit at the sour look Doris made at the mention of their grandson-in-law's name. He patted her on the hand. "Yes, we all know well what you think of him." Doris gave him a look. "Oh, no worries," Glenn continued. "I don't think he was the best man for her either, but... he's done all right by her, hasn't he? She seems happy enough."

"I suppose...."

Glenn reached for the cup and drank deeply. "I swear," he said. "When you make my tea it's always best."

"I heat the cup," Doris said. "The English way, you know. Your mother showed it to me when I was a young bride. And I suppose I always put an extra teaspoon of honey in."

"You are good to me," he said, a bit sadly, staring out the window. "It's a beautiful spring, isn't it?"

"It is," she said. "You'll be out and about soon, enjoying the garden."

A shadow crossed his face then. "I don't know about that," he said. He looked at her intently. "I don't think I want –"

"Drink your tea, dear," Doris said. "I don't want you upsetting yourself."

"Of course," he said and drank.

Doris stood and crossed to the window. The grounds on this side of the house were pristine. Manicured beds of spring flowers and budding trees, and fresh, bright green grass. From here everything looked normal, perfect.

She turned. Glenn set his cup aside. "I think I'll nap," he said. "I'm still feeling a bit sleepy."

"You do that," Doris said. "I'll just go downstairs and catch up on some phone calls." She paused at the door. "Sleep well, dear."

"Thank you," Glenn said, settling back. "Thank you for – everything, Doris."

She smiled at him. "My pleasure." She put her hand on the doorknob. As she walked out she left the door open half way.

When she reached the staircase, she removed her shoes and held onto the banister with one hand, her shoes with the other and once again stepped over the trip wire. She walked quickly and quietly down the stairs to the landing. There she picked up the stack of heavy books. She turned her head toward the second level of the house and screamed, "Oh, my God!" Then she dropped the stack of books down the first flight of stairs. They tumbled, making a thumping racket as they fell. "Help!" she cried pitifully. "Help me! Glenn! Glenn!"

She sat down on the floor of the landing, replaced her shoes and arranged herself in a sprawled position as she heard Glenn's door crash open and his unsteady steps clumping down the hallway upstairs. "Doris!" he cried. "I'm coming!"

She looked up to see his approach at the staircase, the panic in his eyes when he saw her lying there. He was already listing sideways a bit from the tea. He didn't see the wire stretched across the top step.

She pushed herself up to a sitting position against the wall as his body crashed onto the landing. The wire had done its job. And the drug finished it.

32

Bernie reached the cottage door, pulled open the screen then pushed on the wooden door but was met with resistance, the bottom of it thudding against something. Bernie pushed again and heard a soft moan. Her heart beat in her chest as she looked through the tiny, diamond-shaped window and saw her sister lying on the wooden floor. "Bobbi!" she called out. She put her face to the window again and saw her sister had roused and was looking up at her, her mouth opening and closing weakly. "Hang on, sister!" Bernie called out through the crack in the door. "I'll go 'round to the porch door!"

Bernie scrambled around the cottage through the thick foliage, cursing herself. How many times had she vowed to cut all this back and create some order? But she and her sister had loved how the trees and bushes hugged the little cabin, sheltering it. She finally reached the back door and pushed her way through, rushing to Bobbi's side. Her heart melted at the sight of her lying there, her chubby legs moving weakly. She was trying her best to sit up, but Bernie knelt beside her and cradled her. "Don't, darling," she said. Her eyes welled as she noted the side of her sister's face drooping slightly. A stroke. "I have to call 911, dear heart," she said gently. "Just hang on."

She began to rise, but Bobbi clutched her hand. "Ora..." she whispered weakly.

"Sister! Please! I have to call-"

Bobbi shook her head, struggling. "No!" It came out in a rush of air. "Noooo-ra! Sh...nnnng..da..da..ja..." She fell back weakly. Now, Bernie was doubly panicked. Nora? In danger? She leapt for the telephone, noting as she passed the kitchen table the tarot cards spread out upon it: the Tower, the Queen of Batons reversed, and Nora's card, the Moon. Her hands began to shake. She dialed 911 and gave them directions and then hung up quickly and dialed Nora's number for the third time that day, frustrated when it went directly to voice mail. She looked at her sister, helplessly, then the cards on the table. She had no doubt in her mind that Bobbi was right, something bad was going to happen to her granddaughter and she had to find someone to help her. As she heard the wail of sirens in the distance, Bernie Pepper dialed Lucien Pike.

33

Nora pulled the Jeep to a halt, gravel spewing out from her back tires as she pulled along the side of the road near the field stone entry to the Waldemar property. As she did so, she heard her cell phone go off and she stuck her hand in her bag and pulled it out, not needing to look at the screen to know whom it was. *Lucien* she thought angrily. Leave it to him to call her back now, when she'd already gone off on her own. She threw the phone down. She'd talk to him when she was good and ready now. The hell with him. She cut the ignition and sighed, leaning back and looking at the roof and chimneys of the big house that stuck out above the many trees that surrounded it, waiting for her anger to abate. She wanted a clear head before -

What in the world was she doing? she thought. What if she was wrong? She'd look like a fool. She sat looking at the stone fence and pillars that marked the property and the winding drive beyond, the manicured grounds stretching right out to the road. Keeping it up must cost a pretty penny, Nora thought, but then the Waldemars certainly had the means. In the case of Doris and Glenn Waldemar, money had married money. Everyone knew that.

Yes, everyone, Nora thought. It was local gossip that Glenn Waldemar and Doris Welch had been promised to one another at a very young age, which Nora thought was just barbaric, but then, in the day was still accepted, she supposed. She sat back in her seat, chewing on her lip. She reached in her bag and took out Bettie's letters, running her fingers over them. So, what if Glenn Waldemar had written the letters? What if he and Bettie Pepper, a girl from a moderate farming family, had been in love? That would have thrown a monkey wrench into the Waldemar and Welch families plans, now wouldn't it?

She pulled the letters up to her nose and sniffed in their dusty, dry scent. But what if she was wrong? The letters were signed simply "-G". That could stand for anything, right? George? Gary? And who was that old guy who had tea with Bernie and Bobbi sometimes? Grayson LaFromoise. He was a cute old man and seemed to dote on the Pepper sisters. Maybe he'd been a beau of Bettie's. She sighed and stuffed the letters back into her bag. It was just like her to go off half-cocked, now wasn't it. When what she should have done was just gone to her grandmother in the first place and fessed up to sneaking around in her dead grandfather's loft and finding the letters. Yes, she thought to herself, that's exactly what she should have done and...she supposed that was what she would do. Right now, before she made an ass of herself in front of Vivian Waldemar-Spruce. That was all she needed. She was embarrassed enough about her ungraceful exit the night of the anniversary party.

Nora put her hand on the ignition and turned the key. The engine started to catch then wound down to nothing with a tired groan. She startled. She never had problems with her grandfather's old Jeep. She'd spent a lot of money having it restored to its original condition and made a point of keeping it well maintained. She turned the key again to no avail. The Jeep was completely dead. She sat there for a moment simply staring, not sure what to think. Then she chuckled to herself thinking what Bernie would say to her, telling her that the Jeep's malfunction was the Universe telling her that she should not have been going to the Waldemar's in the first place.

She reached for her cell phone and scrolled through her contacts to find the number for Gordie's, the repair shop that kept the old 1973 Jeep Comando in shape, but as she reached to push the call button, the phone suddenly went completely black. "Okay, Universe," she said. "I get it, I get it." She pulled out the phone charger and plugged it in, but the phone still remained dark. How could her battery be completely dead? She messed with the phone cable, pulling it out and plugging it back in, and then, from behind her in the back seat Nora heard a rustling.

She turned, sucking in a scream. There, sitting in the back seat of the Jeep were the twins, but they didn't look like the sweet, little well coiffed girls she'd seen before. Their hair and clothing were black with sludge and weeds, and their faces looked like they had been eaten away, holes where their eyes used to be, and teeth glimmering from behind rotting lips. They were sitting close together, holding hands. On each of their heads, a wet, moldering hair ribbon listed to the side.

"It's time," said one, her voice rusty as ancient violin strings.

"There are no secrets that time does not reveal," said the other through her ruined mouth.

The Jeep engine caught then, with a great roar, and when Nora turned back to look, the twins were gone. In their place were two, rounded indents in the padded, vinyl seat. Both were wet with foul smelling water.

34

Lucien hated cases like this. Drunken idiots who got their noses bent out of shape over something stupid (this time a game of darts) and ended up hurting each other. In this instance, one person had ended up dead, an old veteran everyone knew as Sonny Cats because he kept a plethora of stray felines in his old trailer at the edge of town. Unfortunately, Sonny had been an innocent by-stander, until at least, he'd decided to step in between the two punks who'd gotten into a squabble over the dart game. It had started before lunch time, around eleven, early in the day to be smashed and rowdy, but these two had decided the bar was a good place to spend the unemployment checks they'd received that morning. Now one of them was in the hospital, the other one was sitting in the black and white waiting to be driven over to the jail for interrogation and poor Sonny, the good Samaritan who was probably trying to impress the aging bar maid, was lying in the morgue. The only good thing he had to say about any of it was that it had been over by the time he and the other officers had gotten there, the assailant sitting on the floor, crying over his wounded friend, saying how he hadn't meant to hurt him. Wasn't that always the way, Lucien thought. Too little, too late.

Inside his jacket pocket his cell phone rang. He cringed. It was probably Nora calling again and he was fairly certain she would be pissed. She was, and always had been, both understanding and frustrated by his job which could call him out at any hour of the day, regardless of circumstance or holiday or whatever family calamity might be going on. Ashton Bay was a small town, and as such, had a small staff of detectives; himself and two others. John Bascomb, an "old timer" in his early sixties who Lucien was pretty sure was just biding his time until he could retire, and the new guy, a young, overly-anxious veteran just back from a tour of duty in the Army, Marty "Stache" Stanuszak.

He checked the number before answering but didn't recognize it. "Pike," he answered. On the other end commotion could be heard, then crying and then a very distraught Bernie Pepper began to speak.

"Lucien!" she said, her voice breaking. "I need… I need…"

Lucien's heart caught in his throat. "What's happening, Bernie?" he said. "Is it Nora again? Is she-"

"No! Yes! Oh…. I'm sorry, Lucien. Give me a minute." At the other end of the line Lucien heard the sound of Bernie blowing her nose.

"It's Bobbi," she said. "She's had a stroke."

"Oh, my God," Lucien replied. "I'm so sorry! Is there anything- Does Nora know?"

"No," Bernie said, seeming to pull herself together somewhat. "I haven't been able to- you see, we… She hasn't been talking to me for a few days because we…"

Lucien raked his fingers through his longish hair, already feeling frustrated and helpless. "I'll call her," he said. "In fact, I thought she was calling me just now, when you called. We were supposed to-"

"No, Lucien! Listen to me!" Bernie interrupted. "I – we – Bobbi and I, we think- we think Nora might be in some kind of trouble."

"What kind of trouble?" he asked.

"We – I – don't know," Bernie said. "Look, I know you don't believe in-"

"What kind of trouble?" he asked more forcefully this time.

"I can't say for sure," Bernie replied. "But I think its something to do with my missing sister. Bettie."

"What...? How..." he began, then clamped his lips shut. He knew better than to go down that road. "Listen, where is she?" he asked.

"I don't know," Bernie said, beginning to cry again.

"Bernie," Lucien said gently. "Go be with Bobbi. I'll find her and bring her right to you, okay?"

"Please," Bernie said. "Please find her."

35

Stewart was frustrated bordering on angry. He was tired of calling The Pepper Pot trying to get in touch with Nora about what he'd seen on the video footage. He'd thought about showing it to

Bernie and Bobbi, but there was something about them that creeped him out just a little. He suspected it was their age. Not to mention the fact that they really did dabble in things that were – otherworldly. Unpredictable things. Just because he was a paranormal investigator didn't mean that this stuff didn't scare him a little – that was part of the thrill of is, wasn't it? But these women – they were ancient – and showing them something like this – couldn't it give them a heart attack or something, right? He wasn't used to being around folks older than his parents who were in their early sixties. Both sets of grandparents died when he was too young to remember, so he'd never really been around anyone elderly and – well, it just made him a little of uncomfortable.

He had gotten Kat Kalinowski on the phone a few times trying to contact Nora – and he'd wanted to tell her about the video, though he had to admit it was maybe to show off a little. However, he prided himself on being professional and it was only right that he talked to the family that had asked for his help first – and even though that person wasn't Nora. In fact, Nora seemed to be pretty reluctant to deal the whole thing – but it was only right that he showed her first and then let her decide whether to show Bernie and Bobbi.

He was sure Nora was dodging him, and Kat was covering for her. While that made him a little angry, he it admired at the same time. It showed him that Kat was someone who would protect her friend and that said a lot about her. Plus there was the fact that she was so damned....adorable... Stewart shook his head. No time to think about that now, he thought. In fact, he was just going to go hunt

Nora Pepper up on his own. He was tired of calling. He packed up his laptop into a padded duffle and headed out the door.

At The Pepper Pot he pulled into the alley on the side of the building. No matter how he felt about what folks thought of him and what he did, he was sensitive to the fact that the Pepper Pot was Nora's business. Perhaps she wouldn't want him parked in front of her shop for all of Ashton Bay to see. He wanted to start off on good footing with her, show her he was trustworthy, thoughtful. He shouldered his duffle and swallowed his nervousness and headed for the front door.

Inside, Kat Kalinowski was on the phone, her face nearly as red as her hair. When she turned at the sound of the bell over the door, the look on her face was enough to wither Stewart's insides; eyebrows frowning and pretty lips pursed. He pitied whoever was on the other end of the phone line. At the sight of Stewart, her face changed from angry to surprised and back to angry again as her caller droned on. Finally, Kat said, "Fine!" and slammed the phone down. She turned to Stewart, her face still red.

"Sorry about that," she said. "Idiots! What am I supposed to-" She pushed her fingers through her short, spiky hair, standing it up on end making her look like an angry pixie. Disney's version of an angry Tinkerbell. In spite of himself, Stewart grinned. "What?" Kat huffed. "What's so funny?"

He shook his head, trying and failing to wipe the grin off his face. "I- uh – nothing," he said. "Nothing at all." He took a step toward her - only one step. Kat still looked charmingly volatile. "I- uh – I've been trying – "

"To get in touch with Nora," Kat interrupted. "I know. I know. Haven't we all." She sat down on a stool at the large, stainless steel workstation in a huff and picked up a cup that was easily about as big as her head and took a long drink. "Oh," she said, her face coloring. "I'm sorry. How rude." She held up the cup. "Coffee?"

"I – sure," Stewart said.

"Sit," said Kat, indicating the other stool. She busied herself grinding beans and putting water on to boil.

"So," said Stewart. "Your phone call. It sounded-"

"There's some kind of damned trucking strike," Kat said. "We have an engagement party to cater tomorrow night and of course, three damned seafood courses. And no trucks." She placed ground beans in a French press pot and proceeded to pour boiling water on the grounds. Immediately the room was filled with the enticing aroma of fresh coffee. She reached up on a shelf for a ceramic mug. Stewart remembered seeing mugs just like these at the old Pepper sisters' cottage and surmised Bernie must have made them in her pottery studio.

"So, what will you do?" he asked, for a moment caught up in watching Kat, forgetting completely about the amazing footage stored on his laptop.

Kat pressed the strainer down on the coffee pot and poured Stewart a cup of fresh brew. "Cream? Sugar?" Stewart shook his head and reached for the cup. "That's why I was trying to get in touch with

Nora. I told her to take the day off – we had everything handled for tomorrow – but now, with the damned trucking strike, we need to drive to Detroit to pick the seafood up – and my car is too small to do it. We'd need to take her Jeep. Everything has to be packed on ice in coolers and..."

"I have my van," Stewart interrupted. Kat's eyes opened wide in surprise. He wasn't sure how to interpret the look she was giving him and began to stammer. "I mean – I – I have a van – and it's – nearly empty and I could – I could drive you –"

Kat suddenly rushed forward and put her arms around Stewart's neck. As a bonus she also kissed him on the cheek. "Stewart Schmidt, you are a life saver!" she said. She reached under the counter and pulled out a large Styrofoam cup and lid and poured his hot coffee inside it. "If we leave now," she said placing the lid on the cup and handing it to him. "We can be there and back in three hours tops. And I'll pay for the gas!"

Stewart stood, blushing to the roots of his hair, the video of the ghost twins completely forgotten.

36

Nora put the Jeep in gear and crept up the driveway to the Waldemar estate, the smell of the brackish water on the back seat where the twins had been sitting moments before filling up the cab. Her hands were shaking and one look in the rearview mirror showed her that her face was drained of color, her eyes wild looking behind her black framed glasses. Moments before she'd tried to turn the Jeep around and leave but it had stalled out again, refusing to start. The radio had switched on of its own volition, filling the Jeep with the crackling record sound of the old Frank Sinatra version of Pennies From Heaven running at varying speeds. Nora had begun to feel sick to her stomach. Panic gripped her and she reached for her phone, which was still dark and dead, and helplessly stabbed at the power button to no avail, then coming to life in her hand startling her. The screen flickered on and off showing her a moving picture of the dead twins holding hands, mouthing the words of the song along with the radio.

Nora felt the gorge rise in her throat. She got the door open just in time to lean out and heave the hot, acrid vomit into the weeds at the side of the road. Inside the Jeep, the music wound down to silence. She reached in to the console where she always kept a bottle of water and rinsed her mouth, then wiped at her lips on her jacket sleeve. In the rearview mirror her face looked pale and drawn, her stomach and hands still fluttered with fear. Outside the Jeep before her and behind her all was still. A normal, pretty spring day. She put her head back against the seat and closed her eye and tried to breathe. To concentrate on – anything other what had just happened to her.

And then she heard it, the voice of her grandmother, soothing, soft. She felt the comforted suddenly, the way she had when she'd spend the night with Bernie as a child, cuddling in her big, soft bed, her grandmother rubbing her back, telling her stories – and talking about Nora's dreams, the feelings she had, about things that were about to happen. Feelings that hadn't yet been shamed out of her by her mother.... *Don't be afraid*, she heard Bernie saying. *Don't be afraid to reach out, ask what is needed... use the gifts you have, Nora, for they **are** gifts. Not something to be afraid and ashamed of...*

Nora opened her eyes and looked hesitantly around her. On the seat next to her, the packet of letters peeked out of her bag. She reached over and pulled them out. Her hands shook a little as she lifted them and pressed them to her heart. She and closed her eyes and took a deep, cleansing breath. Okay, she thought to herself, I can do this. She pictured her grandmother and aunt as she'd seen them so many times giving a customer a reading or just getting in synch with one another, trying to reach out to a world that was beyond the physical. A world Nora was not sure she believed in, not in her rational mind, anyway. In her heart, thought, she did know. All the things that had been happening to her lately- she didn't think she couldn't deny it any longer. Perhaps there were senses beyond sight, sound, taste, touch and smell. Sense that she had access to, just as her grandmother had always told her.

As she focused, searching for the stillness within herself, she saw in her mind's eye the loft in the barn. All of the things she was used to seeing there, though, her grandfather's things, were gone. Instead the loft was filled instead with bales of sweet hay on one side and some rusting parts and wooden tools on the other. In one corner a small alcove had been built of hale bales, and an old quilt had been spread on a floor of the sweet-smelling stuff. There, lying on her stomach, her dark, curly hair hanging down over one shoulder was a beautiful, young girl, and when she lifted her face so Nora could look directly at her, she gasped. It was like looking into a mirror.

Spread around her were the letters. The young woman was tracing the signature with her finger, lovingly over the curves of the – G. She seemed to look directly at Nora then, and Nora could see that tears spilled from young Bettie Pepper's eyes. It so moved her that she was surprised to feel tears on her own cheeks. Her heart clenched with love for this girl she had never known with sudden and immeasurable familial love. *"Please,"* Bettie said. *"Please – I want them back."*

"Who?" Nora asked.

"My pennies," Bettie said, and as she did, the edges of her face and body and hair seemed to waver, to melt a little, as did the scene in the loft.

Nora felt panicked again. "Don't go!" she cried, watching Bettie and the loft fade and the roadway and trees outside her vehicle come more into focus.

"I just....wanted them back," Bettie said, and then faded completely.

Nora sat back feeling as if all the wind had been knocked out of her. She still didn't understand what Bettie had meant. Her pennies? Did her disappearance have something to do with money? Nora couldn't imagine that. But one thing was certain. She knew in her gut she'd been right about who'd written the love letters to Bettie Pepper. It *had* to have been Glenn Waldemar. They must have had a secret love affair before Bettie had disappeared. And if that was true, then Glenn had to know something about that disappearance - and she was going to find out what it was he knew. It was time to put an end to the mystery for her grandmother's and aunt's sakes once and for all. And if her intuition wasn't enough for Nora, when she put the Jeep in gear and pulled it through the arched stone gate, she saw the twins standing at the side of the drive holding hands as always, their dark eyes urging her forward.

37

When Lucien pulled up in front of The Pepper Pot, he noticed the white van that belonged to that nut Stewart Schmidt parked in the side alley. What in the world was Nora doing talking to him? Practically every cop in town – and admittedly there weren't a lot of them in Ashton Bay – had either ticketed or arrested him for trespassing at some point, mainly on abandoned properties or private cemeteries, nothing serious. But in Lucien's opinion Schmidt was a nuisance.

He pulled the front door of the shop open and nearly crashed into Kat with Stewart in tow coming out of the Pepper Pot. "Whoa, there, " Kat said, stepping back. Lucien noted that her face was a little flushed. She looked giddy. "I was just locking up."

"Where's Nora?" he asked, noticing that Stewart was ducking behind Kat slightly. Lucien stepped sideways a bit so he had a better view of him. "Stewart," he said nodding.

"Oh, hey, Mister – I mean, Detective Pike."

Kiss ass, Lucien thought.

Kat pushed forward, keys in her hand, forcing Lucien back. She locked the door of the shop. "Your guess is as good as mine," she said. "She took the day off, but normally, you know how she is – she still calls me twenty times a day…"

"Right," Lucien said.

"You're not the only one trying to get in touch with her," she said, talking as she walked, shouldering her bag. "Stewart, her gramma… and I haven't heard from her. I've left her a zillion messages – and you know how she is when she isn't at Pepper Pot – she checks in - wait…" Kat stopped for a moment and looked more closely at Lucien. "What's wrong?"

"Bobbi's had a stroke," Lucien replied. He didn't want to bring up the other part – Bernie's intuition that something had happened to Nora. That was best kept to himself, he thought.

"Oh, my God!" Kat exclaimed. She put her hand on Lucien's arm. "Check the – well, you know where to look for her as well as I do. If anyone can find her, you can," she said. "And when you do, tell her not to worry about a thing. I'll have tomorrow's catering all taken care of. She needs to be with her family. And Stewart will help me, too, won't you?" She turned to him, and he looked back at her, his mouth hanging open.

"I don't know how to – " he began, but was immediately lost in her blue eyes. "Okay," he said helplessly.

"Call me!" Kat said, as she hurried Stewart toward his van. "When you find her, okay?"

"Will do," Lucien replied, wondering where Nora was. There was one thing he knew about his ex-wife – if neither Bernie nor Kat nor he knew where she was, that meant she hadn't wanted them to know. It also meant that he was going to have a hard time finding out where she'd gone and what she'd gotten herself into.

38

Bernie sat in Bobbi's hospital room, working her hands in her lap as she waited for her sister to wake up. She disliked waiting, and she disliked seeing her sister like this – unconscious and helpless - even more. And she disliked hospitals. Especially this one. It was where they'd brought Charlie's body after the car crash, and it was the last place she'd seen Chance Delacoix alive. Sometimes it still surprised her how much she missed them both. They'd have been so proud to see how Nora had turned out, of the way she'd started her own business and was successful. The kind of person she was, smart, funny, compassionate. And if Chance had been around, there wouldn't have been a divorce for Nora and Lucien. If that man had believed in anything it was true love. He would have talked those young folks out of all that divorce foolishness, of that Bernie was certain.

Truth be told, she was a romantic at heart as well, and that was why there was a part of her that was still so angry with Lucien Pike. She knew he'd loved Nora, so how could he have not known her true heart? Sure, Nora had told her grandmother that the divorce was her idea, that it was what was best for both she and Lucien, to choose to be apart now before things got ugly between them. It was all a load of bullpucky, as far as Bernie was concerned. Ah, they were both stubborn, she thought. Stubborn and foolish. Why anyone could look at the two of them together in the same room and know how they both still felt.

But Bernie had to admit, she understood her granddaughter. Like Bernie, Nora had a hole in her heart, a big, ragged one left by the loss of her father and her mother's betrayal. Not to mention Ivy's mothering, which had been a roller coaster ride for the girl. It was no wonder she had a hard time trusting love. And Nora was hardheaded. About Lucien and about her psychic gifts. She only hoped that she would use them now. The cards indicated she was going to need them, Bernie thought. And soon.

Near her on the bed Bobbi stirred, but did not wake. Bernie was pained to see that the droopiness of the left side of her sister's face had not gone away. The doctor said it might improve or clear up completely – or not at all. It was hard to tell with strokes. It had been a fairly mild one, but they would not know where Bobbi stood until she awoke. Bernie reached for Bobbi's hand, her eyes getting a little misty. Her older sister was her partner, her compadre. They were each other's constant companions, and Bernie knew, though she didn't want to think about it. Someday one of them would end up alone without the other, and as they both got older that day was growing closer and closer.

She reached over and took Bobbi's hand. She thought about the cards her older sister had left on the table, the beginning of the tarot spread. Something, some intuition she'd gotten fairly immediately, had to have upset her enough to cause this – though the doctors said strokes were unpredictable things that could happen for no reason at all. But Bernie knew her sister, and she knew her own gut. And her gut was saying her sister had seen something in those three cards. It was a little dicey for Bernie to interpret, since she wasn't sure what kind of spread her sister had in mind when she'd started laying out the cards, but she could take from those few cards what she could and try to get close to what her sister had seen in her mind's eye.

Nora had long been represented by the Moon card, ever since she'd begun fighting her own psychic gifts. The Moon spoke of emotionality and confusion, and Bernie had to admit, she sure thought her granddaughter was confused – about quite a lot of things, in her humble opinion, but mainly about her heart and her spirit. And until Nora could come to terms with herself – with who and what she really was, well, Bernie feared Nora's life would be harder than it had to be. Bernie and Bobbi had always agreed about Nora's connection with the Moon, which for her meant not knowing her own heart, psychic gifts and intuitions. Not having clarity. Her feeling for the immediate reading was that Nora could be receiving flashes of information that seemed to come out of nowhere, which, she was sure, was probably scaring her more than a little.

The Tower card was always a stinker, representing drastic change, situations that seem to come crashing down, upsets with people and situations – betrayals. Tempers, crises, risks taken that end badly, she thought, and as she did, she felt Bobbi squeeze her fingers gently as though she could hear her younger sister's thoughts. Bernie began to get a bad feeling in the pit of her stomach then. She closed her eyes, thinking about the Tower card and the other one that had been placed directly next to it: the Queen of Batons reversed.

In its upright position it could represent a woman who was intuitive, had good business sense, was socially prominent, attentive to her home and family....but in it's reversed position – that could be someone who was deceitful, arrogant, egotistical...and if she felt threatened, or felt her home or family was threatened, could become as fierce – and dangerous – as a lion.

Bobbi's hand trembled suddenly in hers, and she opened her eyes, looking directly into Bernie's. The connection was instantaneous and electric. And in that moment, Bernie was certain who the Queen of Batons was. She saw a picture in her mind as clearly as if a photograph had been placed in front of her. Bobbi looked in her eyes and nodded weakly. Bernie dropped her sister's hand and started digging through her bag for the darned cell phone Nora insisted she carry in case of emergencies. When she found it, she immediately dialed Lucien Pike.

39

It was all Doris Waldemar could do to muster up some tears. To accomplish her task she'd finally thought about her father, who'd died right after she'd married Glenn. Even thinking about her only child, dead far too young hadn't done the trick. Danielle had been a silly girl with no more sense in her head that her father had. To be honest, she was angry at her for dying the way she had, in a car with her top off, after an evening of drunken partying with her useless husband. Her father, though, she'd been close to him. As close as Doris had ever been to any other human being in any case. David Welch had passed away right in this very house where he'd come to visit his beloved daughter. The heart attach had been sudden and unexpected, coming on at the dinner table. Doris had been sitting right next to him. He'd turned to her and gasped, choking on a piece of roasted pork in the process. The fear in his eyes had been immense, and he'd grasped for her hand. It had happened so quickly that no one had been able to do anything. She hadn't, in any case, and she'd feel the guilt of it for the rest of her life. Capable, bright Doris had been able to do nothing but sit there shocked and helpless while tears poured down her cheeks. After that night, she'd vowed never to feel helpless again. And she wouldn't be helpless now, in the present situation.

After she'd gotten a good stream of salty, hateful tears going, she stepped carefully over Glenn's body. She'd managed to roll it down the lower set of stairs and his body was lying sideways in the hall, his bare feet looking thin, pale and pathetic sticking out the legs of his expensive silk pajamas. She planned to dial 911 and to sound as much the distraught and helpless elderly woman as possible. Up on the landing, old Mister Waldemar's law books had put back where they belonged and the trip wire had been removed and disposed of in the trash bin in the garage. She'd even oiled the lower rungs of the banister she'd attached it to with Olde English Scratch Cover to hide any possible marks the wire had left on the wood.

However, as she began to dial the front door chimes sounded, the brass bells echoing through the house startling Doris. She glanced over at Glenn's body and was thankful that the old, stout front door was still in place, that it hadn't been replaced with carved door inset with several leaded glass windows that Vivian had been lobbying for the past few months. From the stoop outdoors the front hall was hidden from sight. She hastily made her way to the formal living room and peeked through the drapes. There in the driveway was that Pepper girl's green Jeep. What in the world was she doing there? Perhaps, in the ruckus at the party some of her things must have gotten left in the kitchen. Doris shook her head in disgust. The help never knew their place anymore. Showing up without calling first. Coming to the *front* door. She sighed impatiently then pushed the button on the intercom. "Go 'round to the kitchen door, please!" she said into the speaker then released the button and walked away not waiting for a response.

Doris met the girl at the kitchen door. She was taken aback once again at just how much she resembled her great-aunt, Bettie Pepper, albeit with a long, white streak in her hair that began at her right temple and wound down over her shoulder. Probably some fad that was "in", Doris supposed. Who cared whether it looked good as long as it was the current fashion, eh? she thought to herself. But then, the Pepper women had never been….refined, had they?

As Nora stepped through the door a bit hesitantly Doris gestured to the kitchen. "I'm not sure what you might be missing," she said. "I know the evening was…upsetting, to say the least. But you're welcome to look around the kitchen for anything you might be –"

"Oh," Nora interrupted, some confusion in her voice. "I – I'm not missing anything." She was clutching her shoulder bag protectively. Doris lifted her chin. She disliked timid women. And this one certainly seemed to be one of those.

"I'm actually here to see Mister Waldemar," Nora said, a bit more boldly. "I realize he's just back from the hospital, and probably needing his rest, but it's –"

Doris stepped closer to Nora, blocking her at the entryway. "I'm afraid that's impossible," she said crisply.

"Missus Waldemar, " Nora said, this time stepping closer to the older woman, forcing her to take a step back and a seed of anger to bloom. "It's important and – I won't take much of his time, if you could just–"

"What could you possibly have to discuss with my husband?" she asked.

"My – my aunt. Bettie Pepper," Nora said boldly. "I – think – I *believe* – he might know something about her – disappearance."

Doris arched an eyebrow. "Do you?" she said. The girl certainly had developed some guts since she was a child. Doris was remembering suddenly how upset she'd been to learn that Vivian had befriended the Pepper girl when they were teens. And how glad she'd been when they'd parted ways. She smiled ruefully to herself. It hadn't been hard to steer her granddaughter toward the handsome Daniel Spruce. And he'd been just starry-eyed enough to be manipulated.

"Yes," said Nora. "Missus Waldemar, I'm not here to upset you, I just –"

Doris forced a smile. She reached out and touched Nora on the arm. "Nonsense, dear," she said. "That whole thing was – such a tragedy for your family. Why, the whole town was upset over it, I remember it well." She pulled Nora in and shut the door behind her. "Please, my husband is resting right now, but…" She made a show of consulting her watch. "He asked me to wake him in twenty minutes. Perhaps you can wait that long? I'd be happy to fix you a cup of tea."

Doris watched as the young woman let out a sigh of relief. "Yes, thank you," she said. "A cup of tea would be – very nice."

Doris smiled to herself, patting herself on the back for her forethought. She hadn't been sure when she'd prepared the tea for Glenn whether just the one dose would work on him, so she'd readied a second cup, the drug and buckwheat honey already measured out in the bottom of the mug. It was sitting on the edge of the counter right by the stove. All she needed to do was fill it with the hot tea and stir it thoroughly. "It is a cure all, isn't it, dear?" Doris said sweetly as she turned to fill the kettle.

40

Stewart couldn't believe his luck. He'd been nervous at first, but as they drove, he and Kat chatted away as if they'd been friends forever. He was especially happy to learn that Kat was interested in what he did – and that despite her best friend's feelings on the subject, she was a pretty regular customer of Bernie and Bobbi Pepper and their card readings. She also loved watching ghost hunter shows on television and she said, being able to talk to him about it felt like a big relief. It was just something she couldn't talk about with Nora.

They'd picked up the seafood and placed it in ice-filled coolers and were heading north, back toward Ashton Bay. They'd been so busy getting to know one another, that the subject of the evening at Bernie and Bobbi Pepper's cottage surprisingly hadn't come up yet. They'd fallen into a comfortable silence, Stewart driving and Kat watching the scenery pass by. Comfortable silence, he thought. It was such a – good thing. He was normally so nervous around people – well, women anyway. Especially ones as pretty as Kat Kalinowski, especially pretty ones he - *liked.*

As if she could read his thoughts, she turned to him, and he was struck again by her pixie-like beauty- fair skin, bright red hair, a few freckles scattered across her nose that unlike most freckled folks, she didn't seem the least bit self-conscious about. "So," she said. "I have to admit, I was a little disappointed in myself the other night. At the Peppers'."

Stewart furrowed his brow. "Disappointed? How do you mean?"

"I seem to have missed a lot," she said. "And Nora wasn't – very forthcoming."

Stewart gave Kat a thoughtful look. "You want to know something weird?" he said.

"What?"

"None of us have really talked about what happened that night."

Kat turned in her seat, as best she could restrained by the safety belt. "You mean, you haven't talked to Bernie and Bobbi since that night?"

"Nope."

Kat looked confused. "But… isn't it, like, routine to meet with the client after one of your – investigations and, I don't know, discuss what happened?" She blushed. "At least that's how they do it on television. Not that I'm saying, you know, that you're –"

Stewart grinned. "It's okay," he said. "That part is spot on. I do normally do that, but this time – I don't know. I got distracted – and then, well, here we are."

Kat gave him a warm smile that made Stewart tingle down to the tips of his toes. "Yes, here we are," she said.

"There was something..." Stewart began, then got an idea. "Hey," he said, signaling as they came up on an exit off the highway. "Do we have time to stop for a coffee? I have my laptop in the back and – there's something – something crazy from that night I want to show you. You're not going to believe it."

"You know we have an awful lot of expensive seafood in the back on ice, right?"

"Right," Stewart replied. "But let me just ask you this – do you believe in ghosts?"

Kat's expression said that she was curious. "Okay," she said. "We've made good time. We can stop for a coffee."

"Great!" said Stewart, excitement building in his stomach. "I can't wait to show this to someone else!"

"Someone else?"

"You!" Stewart corrected. "I can't wait to show *you*."

41

Nora rolled over on the hard ground, wincing in pain. She hesitantly tried opening her eyes, but found that her right one was glued shut with a combination of dirt, and, she thought her own blood judging from the pain in her head. She reached up and gingerly pressed on her temple, and sure enough, found there was a gash there about two inches long. It seemed to have stopped bleeding, for the most part, but was still a bit sticky. She pulled herself up to a sitting position. Her whole body ached as if she'd been pummeled all over, one rib feeling particularly tender. Around her everything was dark, and wherever she was, it was chilly and a bit damp. She shivered.

She felt around her, pulling herself to a cement or stone wall that was close to her, and propped herself up against it. What in the world had happened to her? Where was she and how had she gotten here? The last thing she remembered was sitting in the kitchen with Doris Waldemar. She'd made tea for Nora, which she thought had been a little bitter, but Doris had explained it had a good deal of buckwheat honey in it – hence the slight bitterness. She'd been hugging her shoulder bag in her lap, hoping the letters within it would give her the courage to ask Glenn Waldemar the things she wanted – needed – to ask.

She'd been nervous with Doris Waldemar, she remembered that, because Doris had always made her feel uncomfortable. In fact, when she and Vivian were girls she was quite sure Doris had done all she could be dissuade Vivian from that friendship. But Vivian being Vivian – and a teenager to boot – she would not be bullied. In fact, Nora could recall several instances of embarrassment at being flaunted in Doris Waldemar's face, she was sure, to satisfy Vivian's sense of teenaged rebellion.

Doris had been gently pressing Nora as to the reason for wanting to speak with Glenn, but she had been hesitant to tell her – hadn't she? Her head ached fiercely, and she knew she probably needed medical attention for her head wound – especially so soon on the heels of the one that had just finished healing. Where in the world was she? Wherever it was, it was quiet as a stone, and practically airless, like a tomb. The thought made her shiver, and she began to wonder how large the room or chamber was, and whether there was sufficient oxygen in it to sustain her for very long.

That thought seeded panic in her gut, and with one good eye open to the blackness before her, she began to gingerly feel her way around the edge of the room. As she scooted forward a couple of feet, her shoe touched on something soft that gave against it. She took a frightened breath and inched her foot closer to the object and pushed at it with her foot. It wasn't moving, so it definitely wasn't alive – but she didn't relish the thought of it being something – dead – either.

She bent forward toward it, gingerly feeling her way across the cement floor that seemed to be covered with a fine layer of dust or dirt. She took a deep breath and put her hand on the object, immediately breathing a sigh of relief. It was her shoulder bag! She snatched it up and hugged it to her, the letters inside crunching. She started digging in the bag for her key chain upon which she knew she had a small flashlight, or her cell phone. It was so black, she had only touch to guide her, and after several futile attempts at digging around in the massive bag – and telling herself again this was one more reason to scale down – she finally dumped the whole thing on the floor between her legs and one by one started replacing items back in the bag, identifying them with her fingers. Check book, change purse, wallet, several lipsticks, a nail file, a smattering of loose papers which she knew were receipts, some hair pins, a bottle of acetaminophen, baggie with a few latex gloves, some antibiotic cream and band-aids in it which she always packed in case she cut herself when she was at a job – but no keys and no cell phone. In the absence of both, Nora felt fear twist in her stomach like a knife. In the dark and chill, she began to shake in earnest. Doris...the tea... Nora began to tremble.

She closed her good eye, wrapping her arms around herself to control the shivering. Okay, she told herself, breathe. Think. What happened? What happened? She felt tears sting the backs of her eyes. Don't, she said to herself, don't cry now. You have to *think*! You have to *pay attention*! "Okay," she whispered to herself in the dark. "You were in the kitchen. You were drinking tea. Doris was ... Doris was..." Nora sucked her breath in. She remembered sitting across the table from Doris – Doris who was not drinking tea.

The older woman had been pushy about why Nora had come to the estate. Nora was getting antsy – she remembered that – and getting a little angry, too, about the tone Doris had taken with her. A tone that made Nora suspect that perhaps Doris knew why – or may have suspected why Nora was there – not that she had the letters, but that she'd come to ask about Bettie. And then – then – Nora chewed at her lip and reached up suddenly for a strand of hair, winding it around her finger, her old comfort reflex. As she'd been looking at Doris, Nora remembered, it was as if – as if a dark brown, murky light had surrounded the old woman. Doris' voice then had become...hollow, as if she were speaking to Nora from the bottom of a well, and Nora had felt nauseous suddenly and then...nothing. Until she woke up here. In the darkness, chilly and wounded.

She sat there for a moment, unsure of what to do. Then, feeling she should do *something*, she reached back in her bag and extracted the baggie of first aid supplies. She stretched a glove over her hand and carefully prodded the wound above her eye, wincing but able to clean away enough of the congealed blood that she could open her eye a bit, not that it helped her see any better in the heavy darkness. Then she squeezed a good bit of the antibiotic cream onto her gloved finger and applied it. Getting the band-aids open was another matter altogether in the dark, but after a few tries, she managed it, covering the wound as best she could.

When she returned the baggie to her purse, she heard a soft rustling sound coming from the inside zippered pocket she'd forgotten about. For an instant, her heart soared. She felt for the zipper inside and raked it open. There in the pocket she found the box of wooden matches she kept to light Sterno cans when she was catering. She extracted the little cardboard box and slid it open taking care not to scatter the matches on the floor in the dark. With shaking fingers she grasped the matchstick and slid the box closed. With her opposite hand, she felt along the side of the box to locate the rough striking strip.

The match flared to life, revealing a small room built of cement block. The floor was filthy with black shards of coal and coal dust. She held the lit match gingerly, knowing she had only seconds to take in her surroundings, and as she turned look behind her, to determine the size of the room in which she was imprisoned she sucked in her breath and her heart began hammering in her chest. There, propped up against the wall near the boarded up coal chute was the completely decomposed body of a woman in a green dress gone black with mold. Her dark curly hair lay in matted clumps on her shoulders and the cement floor. As the match went out, singeing Nora's fingertips, she let out a bloodcurdling scream. Nora had found the long lost Bettie Pepper.

42

Doris sat quietly and let the sweaty, young minister hold her hand. He was new to the church, and though Doris sat on the advisory committee, she had never really liked him. In the case of replacing the aged Minister Foster, however, who'd finally had to go to a nursing home, the majority vote had prevailed. This young man, Jonathan Drake, was too eager to please in Doris' opinion, a fence sitter who tried to make everyone happy and she couldn't bring herself to respect him. However, she let him sit beside her, doing his best to console her while the paramedics removed her husband's body from the house. She had to play the part that was expected of her.

So, she let Pastor Drake give her a poorly made cup of tea that was much too weak and suffered through his asking her repeatedly whether he wanted her to call Vivian, or whether there was anyone she would like to come stay with her until her granddaughter could make it home from Chicago. She'd refused him, of course, and she'd call Vivian in her own good time. After all, she had other things to attend to, hadn't she? Right now all she wanted was for everyone to leave and have the house to herself.

While she half-listened to Drake pontificate on death and grief and God, she wondered if the girl had come to yet. She'd taken a nasty crack on the head when she'd rolled down the stairs and landed on the cellar floor. She'd been heavier than Doris had expected – heavier than Glenn, in fact – even though she was slim. Well-muscled, Doris thought, like she was herself. Had to respect that, hadn't one? A person had to work hard to develop a strong body. She knew that well, didn't she, and thank goodness for it, considering the situation.

Not that she was worried about the girl waking up and making a ruckus. No one would ever hear her. While the coal cellar was attached to the basement proper, it didn't actually sit under the house, but was attached to it by a tunnel about twelve feet long. There was a thick door on the coal room, and another at the tunnel opening in the cellar. When Doris first came to the estate as a young woman, there had been a door to the coal chute outdoors. It had been set into a cement foundation on the side lawn. There had been a rough, dirt driveway on that side of the house as well, near the old kitchen. Coal deliveries could be made without disturbing the inhabitants of the house.

However, old Mister Waldemar, Glenn's father, being the progressive man that he like to think himself to be (and likely for the attention it gained, Doris suspected, he always had been a blustery sort), had the coal furnace removed in 1927 and become one of the first customers in the county to have a new Honeywell natural gas furnace complete with thermostat installed in the mansion. After he died in '36, this was after she and Glenn had gotten engaged, his widow had the outside access removed. In 1937, in anticipation of her son's wedding, she'd had a draughtsman who'd worked and studied under Frank Lloyd Wright in Chicago design and build an outdoor courtyard with a thick cement and flagstone floor, seating and a covered portico. The coal chute doors had been sealed and bolted, and the tunnel door locked after that. Everyone had forgotten about it. Except Doris. In other words, the girl could scream all she wanted and no one would ever hear her. Just like no one had ever heard that tramp, Bettie Pepper, screaming.

How long had it taken her to die? she wondered as the pastor droned on. Days? A week? More? She'd been young and strong, too, but without the backbone Doris suspected her grandniece to have. No, Bettie had been beautiful, too kind and ineffectual in the end. What had she expected? Doris wondered. That her silly dreams of being with Glenn – and the twins – would ever come to fruition? That Doris or Glenn's mother would allow that to happen?

Doris pulled herself fully back to the present as the pastor's monotonous yammering stopped and he looked up to see a uniformed police officer poke his head into the room. "Missus Waldemar?" the officer said.

"Yes?" She extracted her hand from the pastor's sweaty one thankfully.

"We have Mister Waldemar's bod- I mean, your husband – in the ambulance." He came into the room, and stood before her, his hat respectfully in his hand. "I understand the coroner informed you that because your husband passed at home, we do need to do a brief autopsy."

Doris looked away and dabbed at her eye with a linen handkerchief. She thought about the drugs. "His – heart," she said. "He'd only been home for…"

"Yes, m'am," the officer said. "I understand."

"Is that completely necessary?" Pastor Drake spoke up.

"Yes. I'm sorry. I know this is – upsetting."

Doris cleared her throat. "I – completely understand," she said, turning toward the officer, her back to the pastor. "The – morgue – they will notify me as to when I can contact the funeral home? To arrange for the funeral?"

The officer stepped forward and pulled a leather folder from his pocket. He opened it and extracted a business card and handed it to Doris. "I'll be happy to call you personally," he said.

Doris took the card and glanced at it. She offered a sad smile. "Thank you, Officer Meyers."

"Of course, m'am." He stepped back and tipped his head. "Again, we are very sorry for your loss. Mister Waldermar was a kind and generous man. The community will miss him."

"Indeed," Doris replied. "Indeed they shall."

43

Lucien was getting worried. Even thought he and Nora had been apart for some time, he still knew her habits pretty well. It wasn't like her to just disappear like this – especially dodging calls from Kat at The Pepper Pot. Even when she was upset, she was responsible about her business. When she was upset, though, he knew she sometimes liked to go off on her own for a few hours. When she did she favored the Eastern Michigan shore and would walk for hours or just sit on the beach thinking. Since the weather was getting warmer, he thought that maybe that was what she had done, headed north along the shore – or south along Michigan's Thumb to find a good place to work out whatever it was she was going through.

He supposed he should have asked Bernie or Kat a little more thoroughly about what or if Nora had been particularly worried about anything, he scolded himself. Since the night of the incident at the Waldemar's he'd been a bit worried about her himself. He thought back to their meeting at the bookstore. There'd been a look in her eyes – what it was, he hadn't been sure. But, he admonished himself, he hadn't asked about it either. They seemed to have made an unspoken pact between them to remain friends but…not to get too close, too personal. Now, with her apparently AWOL, he was feeling guilty for not listening to his gut and asking her about what was bothering her. Additionally, he felt guilty for not returning her call promptly as he'd promised. Sure, he'd had a case, a serious one. But couldn't he have taken two minutes to just check in with her? How many times had they had that argument?

He thought again about the file he'd left lying on his desk. The Bettie Pepper cold case. He hadn't had a chance to read through it, which he'd wanted to do before talking with Nora. He wanted to put some fresh eyes on the notes and photographs to see whether he could find any holes in the case or avenues that hadn't been investigated. The Peppers had been through so much sadness and loss. He didn't want to add to it if there was nothing in the file worth pursuing.

Lucien remembered how horrible it had been for Nora losing her dad and her beloved grandfather within a year. She and Lucien had been engaged, and losing both, there had been no one to walk her down the aisle at their wedding. So, they'd forgone that part, walking together to meet the pastor who'd married them outdoors on the Pepper property. Regardless, on that special day Lucien had known that the tears in Nora's eyes hadn't been wedding tears alone – they had been tears of grief as well.

Bernie had been a wreck, too, after her son and common-law husband had died, isolating herself - even from Nora - and leaving her to deal with Ivy on her own. Ivy Barrette-Pepper had been a piece of work, for sure, probably still was. Lucien made a point of steering clear of her. She'd gone through the motions, but it hadn't taken long for her to start seeing her lover openly, not acknowledging her part in her husband's death. She'd been his mother-in-law, but Lucien felt no love loss for her. She'd betrayed her husband and her daughter, and the way she treated Nora, her cold aloofness still angered Lucien.

He thought about his own family, his parents, Big Joe and Lucinda Pike, who lived on the northwestern side of the state near his brother Joe and his family of rambunctious kids, and his sister Callie who was an English professor at Northern Michigan University. He wished they'd lived closer to them when he and Nora were married so she could have spent more time with them, felt what real family felt like. His mother still asked about Nora whenever he visited, her dark eyes staring into him like two hot coals. It was as if she could see straight through him, straight to his heart. He chuckled to himself a little realizing she probably could. There was a good chance she knew his heart more clearly than he did. She had the *Mashkikiikwe* ways - Medicine Woman ways. How many times growing up had she told him that? Her knowing stare had caused his boy's heart to tremble on more than one occasion, for sure.

It was all such a mess, he thought, between him and Nora. Whenever they saw one another, it was as if there was an invisible wall between them, a set of unspoken rules, what was all right to say, do, feel... She had some of her mother's aloofness about her, no doubt to shelter herself from hurt, abandonment. She'd suffered that enough, he thought. But he wondered if she felt that way, too, whether like him, she regretted what had happened between them. Whether she wanted... Stop it, he said to himself. What had happened with them was in the past. If there had been a time to reconcile, it would have been during their separation, before their divorce. Not now, years after the fact, when they'd learned so well to be without one another.

44

Doris looked at the screen on the cell phone. **19 missed messages**. Who got that many telephone calls? The girl might be safely out of earshot, but her phone kept going off, and Doris still hadn't been able to figure out how to turn the damned thing off. To add insult to injury, it didn't just ring like a normal phone, but seemed to go off playing various strains of music or making odd series of pings and dings and boops. One ring tone was a meowing cat that was especially annoying, to say the least. Thank goodness she'd left it upstairs tucked away in the folds of clothing in her sweater drawer while the policemen had been in the house. They would have undoubtedly asked questions about the ringing phone for sure. About why she wasn't answering it – especially in the wake of her husband's death.

She slid the slim phone in the deep pocket of her cardigan alongside the keys to the girl's vehicle. After she'd gotten Nora into the old coal cellar, Doris had gone out and moved her Jeep into the old, unused horse stable at the back of the property. No one went back there anymore, not even the lawn man, and she'd had to drive through some considerably high grass. She hadn't known how to drive a stick shift, and the beast of a vehicle had whined in first gear as she'd gotten it up the lane as quickly as she'd been able. She'd worried a bit about the tracks the Jeep's tires had made, pressing the grass down into two wide furrows, but being spring, the grass had popped back into place within an hour. Doris had walked out twice to check. One could never be too careful.

At the top of the cellar stairs, Doris switched on the lights and peered down into the open space. She squinted, stepping down a couple of stairs. Yes, there on the finished floor at the bottom was a smear of blood she'd missed. She held the hand rail and turned around carefully. Under the kitchen sink was a spray bottle of bleach water used to disinfect the counter tops. Doris took it and a roll of paper toweling and carried them downstairs.

In the basement all was quiet. Maybe the girl hadn't come to yet, Doris thought, and maybe she wouldn't at all. Who knew? And would that really be that bad? Doris had no idea the extent of the girl's injuries, but she hadn't looked good. She did want to talk to her though, find out exactly how much she knew, which Doris suspected was enough to get people asking the right questions. And Doris had been through too much to let that happen. It was a shame about Glenn, she supposed. He had been – a kind man but, she thought, a bit misguided. A little too...emotional in her opinion. While she'd respected Glenn's mother a great deal, and did whatever she needed to do to get and stay in the woman's good graces, she felt the Waldemar matriarch had been much too soft on her son. Let him get away with too much. Why, if Eliza and Glenn's father had had a firmer hand, the fiasco with Bettie Pepper never would have happened in the first place. But then, she thought ruefully, she hadn't she had an iron hand with Danielle? And just look where that had gotten them.

She bent and sprayed the bleach on the floor, carefully wiping it up with a length of paper toweling. She placed the used paper on the floor. She would take it up when she went and burn it in the stainless steel sink then wash the ashes down the garbage disposal. She stood back and surveyed the area again, as well as the stairs for good measure. When she was satisfied, she headed toward the back corner of the large cellar and pushed the antique library shelf aside revealing the tunnel door.

At the left of the door there was a hook on the wall. From the hook Doris removed the large, ornate iron key and fit it into the lock. She turned it hard. It stuck a little from disuse, making a raspy scraping sound of metal on metal. She pushed the door open and felt the wall for the light switch. Immediately the tunnel lit up with a dull light. Her shoes clicked on the cement floor beneath her feet.

Halfway down the tunnel, she could hear a scrabbling from the opposite side of the coal cellar door, then frantic pounding. "Help! Help me!"

Damn, Doris thought. That answers my question. She sighed and continued walking until she faced the stout wooden door. The pounding continued. The girl was crying, too. Mewling, actually. Well, Doris thought, she must have found her long lost auntie. Doris put her face near the door. "Stop that this instant!" she said forcefully, and the pounding and yelling stopped. Doris put her ear to the door and could hear the girl's ragged breathing. She was terrified. Good, Doris thought. Very good.

"How did you find out?" she asked.

On the other side of the door, the girl went quiet. Doris heard a shuffling sound. The girl was leaning on the door. Doris could almost feel her hands on the wood on the other side, feeling for a handle, anything. But there was no handle on the other side. Doris had taken care of that years and years ago. "I asked you a question," Doris said. "How did you find out?"

"Let me out!" Nora screamed.

Doris was already losing her patience. She was exhausted with all she'd gone through already that day. She'd thought the whole matter had died along with Glenn, but somehow, somehow this girl had found out – something. Enough to hurt her in any case, Doris thought. From the other side of the door, the girl began kicking the wooden door. It rattled a bit on its hinges, but the thick wood and iron hasps did not budge.

"What the hell do you think you're doing?" Nora screamed. "Let me out! Let me out!"

Doris leaned closer to the door despite the intolerable racket. She cleared her throat. Her voice wasn't all it had been. "Do you want me to open the door?" she asked loudly.

The pounding stopped. Doris heard the girl sob. "Y-yes," came the reply.

"Then answer my question," Doris said. "And I'll let you out." She took a deep breath. "Now. How did you find out? Tell me."

The silence on the other side of the door seemed to last a long time. Doris had to strain her ears to hear the quiet reply.

"No."

45

Kat and Stewart sat in the back booth at the little donut shop they'd found just off I-75 North. Stewart was sitting in the corner with his back to the wall firing up the laptop. Kat leaned forward. "Just tell me," she said.

"Nope," Stewart replied, not taking his eyes off the computer screen. "This is one of those things you have to see to believe. And actually," he glanced up at her. "I guess I wanted someone else to see it to make sure I wasn't seeing things."

"So, this could just be a figment of your imagination?" Kat grinned at him.

Stewart raised an eyebrow.

"Or a way to get me alone in this fine dining establishment?"

Stewart stopped what he was doing and looked at her over the top of the computer screen. Was she flirting with him? He felt the heat in his face and became flustered, accidentally brushing the ESCAPE button. The screen blackened for a moment and stopped loading, taking him back to the welcome screen. "Shit!" he exclaimed.

Kat held up her hands in surrender. "Okay," she acquiesced. "Maybe not…"

"No! I mean – yes –" Stewart floundered.

Kat chuckled at him then leaned forward and put her hand on his arm. "Stewart. I'm just giving you a hard time." She lowered her voice. "And for the record, that shy thing you do is pretty damned adorable."

Stewart clamped his lips together. If he said anything right now he'd sound like a blathering idiot. But inside his heart did a flip-flop. Kat Kalinowski actually liked him. Wow, he thought, just – wow. "I don't do it," he said. "I really am. Kind of shy."

"Well, it's cute."

"Thanks. I think. You're pretty cute yourself." Kat grinned and Stewart scrolled over to his video program and searched through the files. "Okay," he said. "Here it is." He started to turn the computer around so Kat could view it.

"No," she said. "Hang on." She jumped up out of her seat and snuggled in next to him. "How's that?" she asked.

Stewart blushed. "It's – perfect," he said, and for a minute got lost in her eyes again.

"Um – Stewart?" Kat said, leaning toward him.

"Yeah?" his voice sounded dreamy.

"The video?" She grinned again.

"Oh! Yeah," he said. He cleared his throat. "Yes."

He clicked on a file and it loaded a plain gray screen. At the bottom was the date and time they'd met at Bernie and Bobbi's, their address and last name. There was a white blinking arrow in the center of the screen. "Are you ready?" he asked.

"Press PLAY already!" Kat said impatiently.

"Okay," said Stewart. "Here goes." He clicked the arrow.

They watched the evening unfold together. About ten minutes into the video, Kat sat forward with a huff. "Look at that!" she exclaimed. "It's like I fell asleep or something! Right at the beginning. I missed everything."

"Actually," Stewart said. "You played a really important part. You just weren't aware of it. Didn't Nora tell you?"

Kat looked confused. "Tell me what?"

It was Stewart's turn to look confused. "Really? She didn't tell you?"

"Stewart!" Kat exclaimed. "I have no idea what you're talking about!"

"Better yet," he said. "Let me fast forward. I'll show you."

He clicked on an option at the bottom of the screen and they both watched the video slide by triple time. Suddenly, Stewart sat forward and clicked the mouse again. The video stopped and he pointed to the screen. "Watch," he said, and Kat leaned closer.

"See," he said. "There you are. Looking like you're in some kind of a trance and then... right there!"

Kat's eyes popped open in astonishment as she saw herself on the video suddenly waking and looking directly at Nora, speaking the words that had been a mystery to everyone that night, and then slumping over as Stewart rushed to save her from falling onto the floor.

"Wait!" Kat said. "Stop. Can you – I don't know – freeze that thing?"

"Sure," Stewart said. "But I haven't shown you the-"

"Back it up," Kat said, and Stewart complied. "Okay. Stop. Right there. Freeze it."

"What?" Stewart said. "I don't see what you're-"

169

Kat pointed at the screen excitedly. "My eyes! Look at my eyes!" Stewart leaned in as well, his own eyes opening in surprise.

"They're – dark. Brown, I think!" he said. "On the video!"

"Holy crap!" Kat said. "And my – the voice- that's not my voice!"

"I know," Stewart said. "That's what I was trying to tell you. I think you were a channel. You know, someone who speaks for a spirit. Has that ever happened to you before?"

Kat leaned back in the booth, dumbfounded, and shook her head.

"Okay," Stewart said. "Now for the good part. Keep watching." He started the video. On the screen the ghost twins appeared standing between the Peppers and Kat who were oblivious to them.

"Freeze that again!" Kat said. She leaned forward, her nose nearly touching the screen as she peered at the specters. Then she looked intently at Stewart. "We have to show this to Bernie and Bobbi," she said. "And Nora!"

46

Lucien tried Nora's cell phone again, but like it had several times before it went directly to voice mail. It was the third time he'd tried from his office line since he'd been there. He didn't know whether to be angry or worried. It was so like her to clam up when she was angry – if, in fact, she was angry. But then, she'd always had a hard time talking about whatever she was feeling – especially if she was angry. It had been a problem in their marriage - that they couldn't just argue a problem out and then make up like other couples. No, Nora would bottle it up, keep it all inside. Still waters running deep, he thought to himself. He wondered if she ever had trusted him – or anyone – fully enough to let down her guard, all of it and just...feel.

After going to The Pepper Pot, he'd checked Bernie's studio and cabin, the book shop and the quiet spot in the park that she liked along the Archambault River where three tall pines came together and formed a shelter beneath its limbs. They used to go there and make out, too, he remembered, lying on an old blanket on the soft bed of pine needles. He'd walked along the river for a bit, looking for her when she hadn't been in her spot under the pines, to no avail. So, he'd decided to head to the office and get a look at the cold case file and continue trying to call her. He knew he was trying to stay busy to keep himself from worrying, but it sure wasn't working very well.

He wished Bernie had had more than a bad feeling about Nora being in trouble for him to go on, something concrete. He thought about calling her but he didn't want to worry her right now with her sister lying in the hospital. He opened the folder and took out the initial missing person's report and the photograph of Bettie Pepper. It was a photo of all three girls, Bernie, Bobbi and Bettie posed on the lawn in front of the old house Nora had told him used to stand at the front of the property. Though a bit grainy, he could see that Nora looked a good deal like her aunt. No wonder, he thought, Bernie and

Bobbi were so protective of her. She reminded them of their lost sister. As he concentrated on Bettie's face, he suddenly got the oddest feeling. A chill that ran down his spine. He put the photo down and began dialing Nora's number again.

Before it could connect, the desk clerk stuck her head in the door. "Call for you, Detective Pike," she said. "The woman said it's urgent."

"Thank God," Lucien grumbled to himself, thinking it had to be Nora finally calling him back. He punched the blinking light on his desk phone and pulled the receiver to his ear. "Nora!" he began. "Where in the hell-"

"It's me. Bernie," the old woman said. Her voice was breathy, as if she was trembling.

"What is it?" Lucien said, immediately concerned. "Is it Bobbi?"

"No. No, she's resting. But Lucien – have you found Nora yet? "

"I'm sorry. I haven't."

Bernie began to cry. That, in itself, made the bad feeling he already had in his gut intensify. Bernie was not a crier, not by a long shot. If she was that upset...

"Lucien," she said earnestly. "I know who's going to try to hurt Nora."

"Going to?" he said. "As in future tense?"

"I don't know if it's going to or has happened or what, but I do know-"

"Bernie, I just can't go running off half-"

"Lucien Pike, you listen to me!" the old woman said fiercely. "Nora is in danger! I'm certain of it! That crazy, old Waldemar woman is going to hurt-"

Lucien rubbed at his eyes. He was getting a rotten headache. "*Doris* Waldemar? You're trying to tell me that Doris Waldemar-"

"Yes!" Bernie cried. "She's the Queen of Batons! And she-"

Lucien shook his head. It had been a long day. "Queen of...what? Look, Bernie," he said. "I can't just go busting in on the folks who probably pay half the salaries around here. Especially not on a 'feeling' you have."

There was silence at the other end of the line, but Lucien could feel Bernie's white-hot anger regardless. "Bobbi had a feeling," she said stubbornly. "And you acted on it. That feeling helped you find that little boy alive last year, didn't it. Or have you forgotten that?"

He sighed and closed his eyes. And when he did, he could see his own mother, chubby arms crossed over her ample bosom, shaking her head at him and staring him down with her black eyes. He looked down at the file in front of him. "No," he said wearily. "I haven't forgotten. Listen, I'll stop by the Waldemar place and see if, by any chance, Nora is there. Okay?"

On the other end of the line he could hear Bernie let out a sigh of relief. "Thank you," she said.

"But Bernie, I'm not going to lose my job over your feeling, okay? You know what an ever-lovin' old crow Doris Waldemar is."

"Just check," Bernie said. "Please. That's all I ask."

"Okay," Lucien replied. "You've got it."

The desk clerk flagged Lucien over before it made it out the door. "Another call for you," she said.

"Just take a message, Jenny," he replied, pointing a thumb toward the front door. "I have to –"

"It's Walt Solinski," she said. "Something about a Pepper case? Do we have a Pepper case?"

"Give me that," he said, grabbing for the phone. "This is Pike."

"Listen, kid," he heard Walt Solinski say in his gravelly voice. "I remembered somethin'. I lead I had, but, you know, I was a punk cop. Wet behind the ears. And the Waldemars–"

"What did you say?" Lucien stepped away and held his other hand over his ear to block out the sounds of the squad room.

"Yeah," said Solinski. "There was this kid- damned if I can remember his name, but he was trouble, you know, so stuff he said…could be made up, maybe, maybe not…"

"Walt!" Lucien said. "What about the Waldemars?"

"Yeah, well, this kid said he seen Bettie Pepper and Glenn Waldemar one time out in the woods, makin' out. I was all hot and bothered about getting a lead nobody else had and I went out there on my own to question Waldemar, but I didn't even get close to him. Eliza Waldemar – that was his mother – she called the station. I got in a shithouse of trouble. It just got dropped after that."

"Thanks, Walt," Lucien said.

"I don't know if it's anything but I thought–"

"I have to go!" Lucien said. He slammed the receiver in the cradle and hit the door running.

47

Nora couldn't stop shaking. After hearing Doris Waldemar's angry footsteps retreating outside her prison it had been all she could do to force herself not to cry out, to beg to be let out of the place that really had turned out to be a tomb. After the old woman left, Nora, trying to hold herself together as best she could, lit one of the matches and made her way to the coal chute door. She turned her body as best she could away from the macabre sight of her dead aunt, and then lit a third match and pulled on the handle to no avail. A closer look showed her that it had been sealed shut with several stout bolts. The only way out was the door – and it had been locked tight by Doris Waldemar.

Nora scooted quickly across the floor then, as far away from the skeleton as she could. Now the darkness that had frightened her insulated her from the sight of her dead great-aunt – and Nora had no doubt that was exactly who'd been locked away here so many years ago. The knowledge had slammed into her gut as soon as she'd seen the locks of dead dark curly hair lying on the corpse's shoulder. Had Glenn locked her in here? Or Doris? Or had they done it together? Had she been dead before she was entombed here or... Nora pulled her knees to her chest and hugged them to her, trying to keep her fear and panic at bay not wanting to think about the possibilities. These were questions she feared she might never have answers to – and did she want them?

She had to get out. And she was certain that even if she did tell Doris what she knew – or the little she suspected - the old woman had no intention of freeing her, regardless of what Nora would or would not tell the old woman. Nora's intuition told her that, and for once, she'd listened to it, refusing to answer as Doris had demanded. She would disappear just as mysteriously as Bettie Pepper had.

No one had known she was coming here. And that was her own fault, wasn't it? Did anyone even realize she was missing? Hot tears full of self-blame stung her eyes and rolled down her cheeks. Why hadn't she told Bernie? Or Kat? Or at the very least told Lucien? Left him a voice mail or message? She sighed. She knew exactly why. She hadn't been sure about Glenn. She hadn't wanted to appear the fool if she was wrong. And they would have talked her out of going – especially Lucien.

At the thought of her ex-husband, the tears increased. Would she ever see him again? That had been another reason she hadn't told Lucien. She'd been angry with him, her head full of what she'd read in the letters and the possibility of what they'd meant. She'd been impatient. Wanted immediate action. She'd always been somewhat impulsive, a contrast to Lucien's careful reasoning.

It had to have been his job that had kept him away – she knew that, and knew it was unreasonable to get angry about it. He was proud of what he did, and responsible. But those old feelings, old insecurities had kicked in... the feelings of abandonment, of being forgotten. But Lucien Pike was not her mother, and he was not the father who let himself be overrun by Ivy. Why couldn't she just get over those old feelings? Why couldn't she have just been patient? Given him the benefit of the doubt?

Did anyone even realize she was gone? Most likely not, she thought bitterly. That's what happens when you spend too much time alone. When you isolate yourself. It was what she did, what she had done since she and Lucien separated. She'd been so in love with him. She'd lost herself. And when she'd felt them growing apart – she'd been afraid. She'd run away instead of reaching out, talking with him about it, instead of working things out together. Oh, she had Kat and her grandmother and aunt – but she had to admit, because when you're alone like this, in a situation you might not make it out of, you couldn't help thinking about these things. The mistakes you made. The things you should have done, things you could have done better. She had to admit she'd separated herself from the people who loved her. She saw them on her own terms, let them in, but only so far. She tried, more than ever, to feel as little as she possibly had to.

She rubbed at her arms. She was getting colder. Her head was pounding making her feel slightly nauseous. She turned and pressed her back against the wall and leaned her head against it. The movement made her stomach roll and clench. She had to get help. She pushed herself up, using the wall for stability, groaning in pain as she put weight on her feet. Her right ankle was tender and sore. She bent slowly, prodding it with her fingers. It was swollen and scraped. Then as she stood up again, her head began to swim. She tried taking several deep breaths to keep from passing out, but fell sideways, hitting the cement floor with a thud, jarring her already screaming head. As she lay on her side panting, her eyelids fluttering, she seemed to see a glow emanating from across the room. She blinked, unsure of what she was seeing.

Noooooooooorahhhhh....

Nora blinked again. Against the wall beside the rusty iron coal chute door the skeleton of Bettie Pepper was bathed in a swirling glimmer, like smoke. As Nora watched, her heart in her throat, the skeleton began to fill in, dress and shoes, legs, arms, bosom and neck. Finally, her face framed by long, black, curly locks of hair.

Noooooooooorahhhhh....

She was dreaming. She knew she must be dreaming – or hallucinating from the crack she'd taken on the head which had begun to throb. She felt like she was spinning and knew she was in danger of losing consciousness. And then she heard crying, far off and dreamy. A hollow sound, grief so deep. And she could understand that, couldn't she? Grief? As she opened and closed her eyes, trying desperately to remain conscious, knowing that if she passed out she was one step closer to dire consequences, Bettie Pepper began to speak. *I just wanted them back..... my babies....my daughters.....*

48

Doris was exhausted. She wanted a hot shower and a bowl of soup and then to lie down and get some much needed sleep. However, she knew she should probably call Vivian, tell her about her grandfather's tragic *accident* – or could she let it wait until morning? She wondered if the news media had gotten a hold of the information that one of the town's most generous benefactors had died. She wanted to believe she could rely on a bit of privacy, be given a little time – at least until the morning - after all, hadn't the Waldemars been constant and generous supporters of both the police and fire departments of Ashton Bay? As well the hospital? That afforded her a bit of consideration and more than a little respect, didn't it?

In the study she poured herself a stiff scotch. A glass of wine just wasn't going to do it this evening. Outside the sun was beginning to set. Doris stood at the window and stared at the barren garden surrounding the pond. The smile that touched her lips was hideous in the fading light. So, the Pepper girl thought she wanted to know the truth? Maybe, Doris thought, I should tell her. Every gory detail. She swallowed her scotch and poured herself another, the heat from the liquor warming her belly and making her feel a little reckless. Yes, that was exactly what she'd do. She and Nora Pepper could have themselves a little story time before bed. She wondered which one of them would sleep better afterward. Doris laughed aloud at that. My, she thought, my sense of humor is still intact.

She made her way to the cellar and pushed Old Waldemar's library case out of the way again. She was glad she'd thought to use the case to hide the tunnel door. Just in case. One could never be too careful – that was her motto, wasn't it? The case had gone into disrepair and Doris had never liked it anyway so it had gotten consigned to the basement. Its shelves harbored some dusty old jars and boxes. There were small iron wheels at the bottom of each leg of the cabinet, making it easy to move. After moving it to the side, she unlocked the door then fetched old Mister Waldemar's wheeled leather desk chair down tunnel, avoiding some old lumber and tools that were stacked to one side. She parked the chair outside the great wooden door. Her former father-in-law's cast offs were certainly coming in handy, another thought that made Doris chuckle to herself. After the chair was in place she set down the bottle of scotch and her glass, which she'd brought downstairs with her. She might be down here for a while, she thought, and she was damned well going to be comfortable.

There were no sounds coming from behind the door. Doris sat down and poured herself two fingers of scotch. She took a sip. It was good scotch, Glenmorangie Quarter Century. At over six hundred dollars a bottle, it certainly should be excellent, she thought. She leaned toward the door. "Yoo hoo," she called. "Are you awake, darling? Ready to chat with your old hostess, eh?" She chuckled again. She certainly was in good spirits, considering. She felt a freedom, with Glenn dead and the Pepper girl locked up. Back in control. She felt a weight had been lifted from her shoulders.

She listened at the door. Still nothing. "Let's not be rude, now," she said, feeling anger itching in her belly.

Silence.

"Nora!" she yelled. "Nora Pepper!"

When there was still no answer, Doris set her glass down, seething. Why, she'd come down for a little fun and this idiot girl was ruining it for her. Not even so much as a whimper, no begging or crying. Nothing. Doris set her glass on the floor with a clunk and stood. She strode over to a pile of discarded lumber that had been stacked and forgotten in the tunnel. She picked up a short, heavy piece of oak and lifted it to her shoulder like a baseball bat. "Wake up!" she hissed and began to beat at the door with the board.

49

Lily would not stop crying and it was getting on Lucy's nerves. Nothing they'd done had helped them, all their efforts had been for naught. And she was so...tired. She just wanted to float away, up to the sky, the stars, become smaller and smaller until she no longer existed. But she and Lily couldn't leave here. Not without...her. And hadn't they tried so many, many times?

Their despair had begun to fill the beautiful, green pond that had once been so rife with lush, green plants and quick, silver fish, leopard frogs and snails and water lilies. Their despair had killed everything that grew there and the pond was now a place of emptiness, of death, just as it had been when...

That thought made even Lucy quake. She'd always been the strong one, the fearless one. In the darkness, she squeezed her sister's hand. Had she ever told Lily how sorry she was? Hiding that day had been her idea, and Lily always followed Lucy no matter where. Did it matter now? Oh, she was sorry. So sorry. She pulled Lily closer. "Don't cry, dear heart," she said, her own tears catching in her throat.

"You said it was time," her sister said accusingly.

"Yes, I..." Lucy's voice faded. What could she say? What could she say now?

Then Lucy noticed a movement at the edge of the pond, near the old stone bench. She lifted her head and could see that a figure stood there. The figure of a man that seemed to be made of smoke and light. Lucy rubbed her eyes, unable to believe what she was seeing. She squeezed her sister's hand, and both girls' heads turned toward the western side of the pond. The stars seemed to brighten above them, their pinpoints of light raining down on the surface of the water. "Daddy..." Lucy whispered, smiling.

50

Nora felt a coldness brushing her cheek, rousing her. She blinked, trying to focus in the dark. She had a sense of someone leaning over her. "Lucien?" she whispered, her throat dry and raspy. She opened her eyes to see the face above hers, a face very much like her own. There was a smell, a dry, dusty smell, reminiscent of moss and mushrooms. It comforted her.

Noooooooorahhhhhh.....waaaaake uuuuuuupppp....

"Wake up!" another voice hissed beyond the door. Then there was a sharp pounding on the stout wood, making Nora wince, her head feeling as if it was going to split apart. She sat up, clapping her hands to her ears. "Stop! Stop it!" she cried, then looked up in time to see the glowing image of Bettie Pepper fading away into the darkness. Instinctively, Nora reached for her. "No!" she cried. "Don't go!"

"I'm not going anywhere, you twit!" came the answer from beyond the door. "In fact, I thought I'd stay here for a while and you and I would have a little visit. How does that sound?"

Nora scrabbled across the floor fighting back nausea and failing. She turned toward the corner of the room just in time for the acrid bile to come up, burning her tongue and lips. Her stomach heaved. On the other side of the door, the old woman chuckled. "Not feeling so well?" she said cruelly. "Perhaps you need another cup of tea."

Nora's head swung toward the door. "Shut up!" she barked, her stomach convulsing again. She heaved and then sat back weakly, wiping at her mouth which was bitter, acrid, metallic.

"Now, there you go," Doris said. "There's a little spirit."

Over Nora's shoulder, she had a sense of someone watching. She turned her head slowly, trying to keep the nausea at bay. There, just behind her, stood Bettie. Her figure was wavering, glowing a bit in the dark. She was wearing a green dress, sweetly cut with a bit of a drop waist, and brown shoes. Her hair was brushed and shining, held back from her face with a tortoise shell barrette. She looked so young and tender. Nora's lip trembled. Bettie looked into her eyes. They seemed to say *you're not alone.* Nora took in a deep breath. Her trembling seemed to abate a bit, and with it the swoopy feeling in her stomach. She crawled closer to the door. "Missus Waldemar," she said as evenly as she could. "Let me out. Please."

"Hmmm, so formal," the old woman replied. "Since we're now on such intimate terms, you must call me Doris."

"You need to let me out – Doris," Nora said. "My friends know where I am. Eventually they will come here looking for me."

"They will, will they?" Doris said, fairly cackling now. It was a very unpleasant sound. "Well, let's see, I have here....yes, your little cell phone. And I must admit, you are a very popular girl. Over twenty-five missed messages are telling me that perhaps...perhaps no one knows where you are. Is that right, Nora? Messages from....let's see...your grandmother, someone called Kat – is that the annoying ring that sounds like a kitten drowning? And...who is this Lucien? He seems to have called *several* times. Another annoying ring as well. Spanish guitar? What in the world is that? Can't you young people..."

"Let me out!" Nora screamed, slamming the palm of her hand on the door.

"You're in no position to demand anything of me, young lady!" Doris screamed back.

Nora began to cry silently. She felt a hand on her shoulder, light, cold. She looked at the specter of her dead aunt. Bettie shook her head. She put a finger to her lips. *Quiet.* Then she put the finger to her ear. *Listen.*

"I've come here to do you a favor," Doris said. "I'm afraid in your case curiosity will kill the cat, that being what it is, I came to tell you a little story. About your great-aunt and her...little bastards."

"Little...?"

Near her Bettie Pepper seemed to be crying, ghostly tears running down her cheeks. Nora looked at her, suddenly understanding. The twins. The little girls. Bettie's *pennies from heaven.*

"That's right," Doris said bitterly. "My dead husband's illegitimate children. With that trash Bettie Pepper."

"Dead – husband?" Nora sat up straighter. "What did you do, Doris?" she demanded.

On the other side of the door, Nora heard the old woman sigh. "I think I liked it better when you addressed me more formally," she said wearily. "Ah, but no matter..." Nora heard a clink of glass on glass, then liquid pouring. A pause as Doris drank deeply. "Mister Waldemar – had a little accident. On the stairs. It was very tragic. After all, he was healing up so nicely. Too bad he couldn't keep his mouth shut."

Nora began to tremble anew; she rubbed at her aching forehead, trying to wrap her mind around what the old woman was telling her. It was just too much, too much. Again, the pressure on her shoulder, the hand squeezing, giving her comfort. *Listen....*

"Tell me," she began, her voice shaking. "Tell me about - the twins."

"Well," Doris said. "I was right. You did know something. How did you find out?"

Nora hesitated, unsure of what to say, but Doris continued not waiting for an answer, her voice slurring a bit. "Oh, never mind," she said. "It doesn't matter now."

Nora heard more liquid splashing into a glass. "They were a secret," Doris began. "Lily and Lucy. Glenn and I were set to be married within the year. In the fall of 1938. But he'd been seeing your aunt. Your great aunt. Bettie Pepper. What a common name, Bettie. Glenn came to me one night. Said he had to speak to me about a 'serious matter'. By that time, I'd moved to the estate to help his mother prepare for the wedding. His father had died late the winter before. I supposed I could have blamed his – dalliance – on that, on grief, but the truth was Glenn was a weak-willed boy and spoiled, too. And your aunt, I have to admit it, she was – beautiful. I guess they'd been meeting for some time. He told me that she was expecting a child – his child. And then he told me that the wedding was off. He was going to marry *her*."

Outside Doris paused. Probably drinking some more, Nora surmised. She scooted closer to the door and leaned against it to better hear the old woman. She would finally know the truth.

"I went straight to his mother, of course. She was an amazing woman. Iron will. Intelligent. Decisive. More a business head than either her husband or his father had, in my opinion. And Glenn was afraid of her. He needed that, she said, and she taught me well. And she presented a solution."

51

Bernie roused at the sound of her sister's whimpering and went to her bedside. She put her hand on Bobbi's cheek. "It's all right, dear heart," she whispered. "Go back to sleep."

Bobbi's sparse eyelashes fluttered, and she opened her eyes, one of which, Bernie noticed, was still a bit droopier than the other. Bobbi licked her lips. "Dry," she whispered.

Bernie reached for the cup of ice chips on the bedside stand and spooned a few into her sister's mouth. "How's that?" she asked.

"Better." Bobbi blinked her eyes, focusing them in the dimness of the room. Around her monitors still blinked and beeped. "Bernie, hold my hand. Please."

"Of course," Bernie said, placing the cup of ice chips aside and grasping Bobbi's cool, dry hand in her own. It felt incredibly frail, making Bernie's heart ache.

"Come close to me, sister," Bobbi said. "I need to tell you something. It's Nora – she's – she's with – with Bettie. I saw them. Just before I woke up."

"What do you mean?" Bernie said, fear clutching at her. "You think Nora's – Nora's-"

"No. No," Bobbi said weakly. "Please, sister, listen to me."

Bernie scooted her thin bottom onto the bed and sat near her sister. "What is it?" She took Bobbi's other hand in hers as well and then felt the electricity between them, the current that was always there, connecting them, but weaker now, on her sister's end. "Sister, please, you should rest," Bernie implored her, tears springing to her dark eyes.

"Nora is in a dark place. But Bettie is there with her. Watching over her. She's waiting. She's been waiting for…for…" Bobbi's brow crinkled in frustration. "Waiting…for – something. Oh, I don't know what it is for sure!"

Bernie patted her sister's hand. "It's all right, sister," she said. "Just rest, dear. Nora will be fine. Lucien will –"

"Yes, yes," Bobbi said, impatiently this time. "I wanted to tell you. Nora will be all right. But she mustn't go to sleep."

"Bobbi, please– " Bernie clutched her sister's fingers.

"Don't forget, sister," she said. "She can't go to sleep. Then she will be all right. If she does I – I don't know what will happen to her. And Bettie – she'd going to come home, Bernie. She will. I can see it."

"Please, Roberta," Bernie plead. "You must rest, darling."

"I will, sister, but there's one other thing - a box for Nora. I've put it under my bed. Will you give it to her?"

"Darling, you can give it to her when –"

"No," Bobbi said, her voice just a whisper. "I – won't be able to, I –"

Bernie's heart pounded in her chest. "But you're fine, sister!" she said. "The doctor said it was just a mild stroke and you–"

"Please," Bobbi said. "It's – not the stroke. It's been – happening for a while now. The leaving. I didn't want to tell you. So, promise me."

"Of course," Bernie said, crying openly now. "Anything for you. But now you just rest. You rest. All right?"

"I shall," Bobbi said, already closing her eyes. "Sister, I'm so very tired." She took in a deep breath, her chest rising and falling. "Don't forget," she whispered. "Don't let Nora fall asleep."

52

Outside the thick, oak door, Nora heard the sound of more pouring, drinking. She wondered just how much liquor the old woman could hold, for she assumed Doris was, indeed, drinking. "What was the solution?" she asked, wanting to know and not wanting to know.

"She demanded to see Bettie alone," Doris said. "Women are so much better at working these little – problems – out, aren't they?" Doris sighed. "First she threatened to cut Glenn off completely if he interfered. Poor Bettie. She had no idea how weak-willed her lover was. Then Eliza appealed to the girl's sense of shame. What her family would think, if they knew, how her parents – how any parents of a young girl – would be ashamed, disappointed, angry – that they would disown her. She would be alone, with a child – a child that would not, she assured her, be claimed by the father, because the Waldemar family would not allow it. Oh, I was there, she painted a sad, desperate picture for the girl."

"It was her?" Nora asked. "It was it Glenn's mother who locked my great aunt in here?"

Doris laughed. "Oh, my dear!" she exclaimed. "Be patient. We'll get to that."

"Doris, please," Nora said. "Please, just let me out. All this was so long ago, and I'm sure-"

"You don't know anything!" the old woman snapped. "Now, shall I continue, or are you going to insist on interrupting me? If so, I'm happy to go upstairs and go to bed. I've had quite a day!"

"No!" Nora said quickly. "Please, don't leave me alone!" Again, she felt the squeeze on her shoulder. *You're not alone.*

"Fine," Doris said. "That's better." She paused for a moment. "Well, then," she continued. "Back then, there were certain places a girl could go. Girls who were in trouble. They were kept quite private. Eliza offered to pay for Bette's confinement at one of these, quite a posh one, too, for girls from good families who gone – wayward. Afterward, when she'd had the baby the family – the Waldemars – would take charge of the infant. Glenn and I were to be married within months, the to leave for an extended honeymoon in Europe afterward. The third floor would be outfitted for the child. After three of four years, Glenn and I would start telling people that we were going to adopt a child. The estate was so big, and no one ever used the third floor, not even then. The child would never be seen – until we saw fit to make the phony adoption public. And that would be that."

"What about Bettie?" Nora asked.

"I was just getting to that," Doris said. "Bettie would be given a very generous sum of money to 'disappear' for a while. We were going to set her up in Chicago with an apartment, an allowance. We have business offices there and either Eliza or myself would be able to check on her, make sure she was sticking to the bargain. When we'd decided things had calmed down enough here in Ashton Bay maybe twelve or eighteen months later, we would let her come back if she wanted, but she was to have no contact with the child. She was to tell her family she'd run away, but that things hadn't worked out for her. Perhaps invent a failed love affair. For her silence, we agreed to continue paying her a stipend. For the rest of her life."

"But the twins," Nora began.

"Yes, yes," Doris said impatiently. "The cow of a girl turned out to be pregnant with twins. That didn't change anything for Eliza though. In fact, she agreed to give Bettie even more money. I was livid. I didn't want one bastard let alone two! But what could I do? There was an agreement. Between our families. And it was expected of me that I would take Eliza's place in the family, when she died."

Against the door, Nora shifted. Her head ached so badly, and she was starting to get chills. That she had a concussion was now very apparent to her. She took a deep breath and concentrated on staying awake as she listened to Doris' story.

"What we didn't count on," Doris said bitterly. "Was how taken Glenn would be with the girls. They, of course, were adorable. The spitting image of Bettie Pepper, which for me was like rubbing salt into the wound, I'll tell you. I detested being around them, but I had to care for them. Take my turn. Eliza and I – mothering them. We didn't trust hiring anyone to do it. And Glenn, he spent every free moment with them he could. He adored them. He – forgot I existed."

Doris went quiet then. Nora leaned closer to the door straining to listen. There was nothing but silence. Nora's eyes began to flutter closed.

Nooooooooorahhhhhh.....waaaaake uuuuuuupppp....liiiiissssssssstennnnn....

Nora started awake, rubbing her face with her hand. Her skin felt clammy and cold. At her shoulder, the specter of Bettie still hovered. "Help me," Nora pleaded.

Nooooooooorahhhhhh.....

"Oh, no one is going to help you. Just like they didn't help her. Bettie," Doris said.

"What – what happened to her?" Nora said, forcing herself to sit up straight. Her head swam.

"The stupid twit came back is what happened to her!" Doris said forcefully. "What happened to her was her own silly fault!"

"What do you – "

"She came back. It was in July 1942. Hot that year. So hot. She'd taken the train from Chicago to Detroit then hitched a ride in to Ashton Bay with a trucker, can you imagine it? Had him drop her on the road near the estate. For a few days she hid in the woods behind the property, watching. Then one evening I was out on the patio. It was late. Maybe one or two in the morning. This was before we'd had central air installed in the house, mind you, and upstairs the bedrooms were so hot. As I remember, the girls had heat rash and Glenn had made them a little bed on the floor in the library and he'd taken to sleeping on the sofa in there near them.

I was lying on the chaise on the patio. It was still stifling, even outdoors. She was so quiet, sneaky like a stray cat. I didn't even hear her until she was right beside me, looking down at me with her moony eyes. She'd been crying. That was plain. And her dress and shoes were filthy and she looked like she'd been eaten alive by mosquitoes. I remember sitting up, wondering if Glenn had heard anything through the open library windows, and I glanced toward them but all was dark. I asked her what she wanted, and she looked at me with those big, dark cow eyes of hers and said 'I want them back'."

At the same time, next to Nora she heard Bettie's whispery voice. *I want them back...* She shivered.

"I jumped up and grabbed her by the arm and told her to come with me. I took her 'round to the old kitchen door and we went in. I asked her whether she was hungry. Of course I could see that she was and so I gave her something to eat and a glass of milk. She kept thanking me. I remember that. If I were a different kind of person, I suppose that would have put me off what I knew I needed to do. I had to talk some sense into her or she had to disappear. And no one, not even Eliza, could know she was there.

I hid her in the coal cellar. It hadn't taken much convincing to get her to go down there. I said I needed time to speak to Eliza, get her to see reason, and to speak to Glenn. I think the first night she was just grateful to be inside. A night or two in the woods alone will do that to a person, I suppose. I'll never know why she hadn't just run back to her family. But as I said, she wasn't the brightest girl. And

Eliza had laid it on thick. About the shame. What Bettie's parents would think of her. I suppose she believed her, and felt guilty over the pregnancy. So she went gratefully. I gave her an old blanket. She was exhausted. I don't even think she realized I'd locked her in until the next day.

I did try to reason with her, once or twice over the next two days, but she just wailed how she wanted the girls back. That she didn't care about Glenn, she understood he was married now, but she wanted the twins. I wish I could have given them to her. Just given them back and made her leave for good, continued giving her money, but I knew Eliza would never agree. So... "

After a moment, Nora said, "So, you left her in here. To die." She began to shake again, at the horror of it.

"Well," Doris said. "Yes. I did exactly that. And it's why I know you can scream your fool head off and no one is ever going to hear you."

Nora understood what Doris was saying was true. No one knew she was here. And the old woman was not going to allow her to leave. She had too much at stake. She leaned against the door again. She was so tired. Tired and cold. "What happened to the girls?" she asked. "Tell me the rest of it."

"They were four, almost five years old when they – " Doris stopped, and once again Nora heard the clink of glass on glass. The liquid pouring. "There was a grandfather clock in the front hallway, " she said. "Tall, carved. Made in Germany. It was one of a kind. It had gone to disrepair. Eliza was in Europe at the time. She'd visited the clock maker in Freiburg and made arrangements for it to be shipped over to be repaired. There was a secret cupboard built in behind the pendulum case. Quite large. I suppose it was made to store cash or valuables. It opened with a little gold key that was kept in a little drawer built in to the side of the clock. That cupboard was one of the girls' favorite hiding places but not the safest. Once when Lily was almost four, she hid in the clock and none of us could find her. When we finally did, her lips had gone blue from lack of oxygen. Glenn forbade them to ever hide in there again, but children will be children." Doris emitted a dark chuckle. "Especially when provoked"

"Glenn was in Chicago for business. I was alone with them. By the third day I couldn't stand it anymore, their constant crying for their father, whining, not eating what I prepared for them. They were spoiled. Spoiled as Glenn was as a child. I felt as if they had taken everything from me. Them and their mother. Glenn barely looked at me anymore. Not that our marriage was one of love, but of convenience, of business, yet a woman needs certain attentions from her husband – and all of his was focused on the girls. And we hadn't even made the adoption public yet. I knew when that happened, when people started coming around, ooooing and ahhhhing over them... So, we played a game of hide and seek. I knew they were in the clock, I'd made sure of it, with some careful suggestions. I took the key out and locked them in. They didn't even cry. I think, perhaps, they got tired and went to sleep. They just...ran out of air and never woke up."

Nora lay on her side, tears running down her cheeks, imagining the horror of what the older woman had done. To children. Babies.

"Glenn was, of course, out of his mind," she continued. "And he may have been a shallow man, and spoiled, but he wasn't stupid. He cared about the family's reputation, the businesses, the money. We took the clock to the pond together. It floated for a little while, long enough to push it to the center where the water was the deepest. When it sank to the bottom, he howled. Sounded just like a wolf. Then he collapsed and cried like a baby."

"So, the twins. They're in the pond."

"Yes," Doris said. "Quiet as stones."

"You're a monster," Nora said softly.

"I may well be," Doris said.

Upstairs the front door bell chimed, echoing through the house. "Well," Doris said crisply. "I'll assume the evening news found out about Glenn's death. So, I'll be going."

Outside the door, Nora heard the sound of Doris moving things around in the tunnel. "I know you heard the bell," she said. "But once I close the outer door, no one will ever hear you, no matter how loudly you scream."

Nora listened to the *tap tap tap* of Doris' high heeled shoes grow more faint as she walked away. The doorbell chimed again, then there was a thunk and the sound of metal on metal. Then there was nothing.

Behind the thick door she laid down, her throbbing head on her arm. She wouldn't scream. She didn't think she could if she wanted to.

Nora closed her eyes.

53

Lucien looked around and jabbed at the doorbell for the third time. Dusk was falling, and inside the house appeared to be dark. Perhaps, he thought, no one was at home. When he'd pulled up the drive had been empty. The Waldemar's had, of course, a large, heated garage in which to park, so Lucien hadn't expected to see any of their vehicles. More to the point for him was that Nora's old, green Jeep was not in the drive either. He sighed impatiently. What was he doing here? He felt a little foolish, coming here mainly based on Bernie's 'feeling' – but the call from Solinski niggled at his mind as well – what if there was something to it?

Just as he was about to push the doorbell for the last time, he heard the sound of movement behind the door. Then there was a sharp, electronic tick and a voice coming through the intercom beside the massive front door. "Yes? Who is it?"

"Missus Waldemar? It's Detective Lucien Pike. May I speak with you for a moment?"

Lucien heard the click of a lock being turned and the door opened. Doris Waldemar stood, wearing slacks and a cardigan sweater over a blouse. There was a single strand of pearls around her neck. Her white hair was perfectly coiffed, but her face looked strained. She put a hand to her throat. "Detective," she said. "How may I help you? I assume you've heard the news about my husband?"

Lucien frowned. He was pretty sure he could smell alcohol on her breath. "I'm not sure what you mean," he said. "Look, m'am – if I could just come in for a moment and –"

Doris lowered her eyelashes. "He – passed today. Glenn. Here at home. I thought you might have –"

Lucien stepped forward and put his hand on her arm. "I'm very sorry to hear it," he said.

Doris stepped back. "Please," she said. "Do come in for a moment. But I'm very tired." Her head came up and she looked at him in a way that was perhaps supposed to look mournful, but came off, instead, as unpleasant. It was a look that poked at Lucien, at his 'cop brain', as he liked to call it. He got that poke when something felt 'off' to him, and his awareness heightened because it was exactly what he was feeling right now.

"Yes," he said carefully. "I'm sure you are." He followed her down the hall to the library. Doris turned on some lights. She went to an ornate sideboard and uncapped a decanter.

"Would you like a drink?" she asked. "Or are you on duty?"

"I'm fine, thank you," he replied, and watched as she poured herself what Lucien was sure was not her first of the night. But then, she'd lost her husband, he thought.

"Did you say your name was Lucien?" she asked.

"Yes, m'am," he replied. "Lucien Pike. Your granddaughter isn't with you?"

Doris took a drink of scotch. "She and Daniel are flying back from Chicago early in the morning," she replied.

"Perhaps you shouldn't be alone," Lucien said. "Considering."

"Thank you," she said. "I appreciate your concern. But I assure you I'm fine."

About as fine as half a bottle of good scotch can make you, Lucien thought to himself. He looked around the room. Everything seemed in place.

"So, what brings you here, Detective?" Doris asked. "How can I help? You know my husband and I have long been great supporters of-"

"Yes, m'am," Lucien said. "Your generosity is much appreciated. I'm looking for someone, actually. I'm hoping that perhaps you can help me."

"Of course," Doris said. "If I can. Who are you looking for?" She took a seat in a wing-backed chair and looked up at him intently. There was something in her eyes that unsettled Lucien. He turned, placing a hand in his pocket, trying to shake the uneasy feeling.

"Nora Pepper," he said. "I understand she was headed for the estate earlier today." A bluff, he thought, but he would see what came of it.

"Oh!" said Doris. "As a matter of fact, she was here today. Earlier."

Lucien raised an eyebrow. It was information he hadn't expected. "What time was that?" he asked.

"It was – " Doris suddenly turned away and put her hand to her cheek. "I'm sorry," she said. "It was right after – the paramedics had just arrived to take my – take Glenn away. He had a heart attack. On the stairs and – there was just so much happening. Nora had come to retrieve some of her equipment that was forgotten here the night of the anniversary party." Doris' eyes welled with tears.

Lucien felt like a heel. He stepped toward her. "Missus Waldemar, please," he said. "I'm so sorry. Listen, I'll just – " he thumbed toward the front door. "I'll just be going. I'm sorry to disturb you at such a – difficult time. Please forgive me."

"Nothing to be forgiven, Detective," she said, rising. "I understand you're just doing your job. Please, let me walk you to the door."

"No need," he replied. "I'll show myself out."

"As you wish," Doris replied. She took another sip of scotch.

Lucien walked across the library. Just before he reached the door, from behind him he heard the sound of a mewing kitten, a familiar, electronic sound. He turned suddenly, his eyes narrowing slightly.

Doris' eyes opened wide, her hand flying to the pocket of her cardigan. The mewing sound came again. "Oh!" said Doris. "My – cell phone! Isn't that silly?"

Lucien's cop brain fired on all its cylinders. His face was a mask. He'd learned to hide his thoughts and feelings well in the eight years he'd been a detective. He tipped his head at Doris. "I'll let you get that," he said.

Doris looked down at the phone in her hand. "It's quite all right. It's gone to voice mail," she said.

"In any case, I'll show myself out," Lucien said. "Good night."

"Good night," she replied. "I'm sorry I couldn't have been more help to you."

"Of course," he replied, giving her a steely smile.

In the hall, Lucien pulled his own cell phone from his pocket and scrolled to Nora's number, punching the call button hastily. From behind him, in the library, he could hear the strains of Spanish guitar. Brian Adams. Have You Ever Really Loved A Woman. He turned on his heel, his eyes meeting those of Doris Waldemar.

54

Doris was indignant over the way she was being treated – and she swore she would have Lucien Pike's badge over it. He'd at least allowed her a glass of water to soothe her raw throat. She was more than a little embarrassed over the way she'd reacted, hollering until her voice was nothing more than a whisper. What could she expect? She'd worn the poor thing out today, hadn't she? Telling the Pepper girl the long, sad story about Glenn and Bettie's ill-fated love affair? And then this? This – travesty? Being chained up like a common animal?

He'd fairly ripped the girl's phone out of Doris' hand. She remembered then. They were married. The Pepper girl and Pike, or at least they had been. So his inquiry hadn't been completely – professional. She could hear him on the second floor of the house, opening and closing doors, calling out for Nora in vain, and then suddenly there was quiet. She figured he must have found the door to the third floor and gone up there. Well, she thought smugly, he certainly won't find anything up there. That hadn't been used since – well since Lily and Lucy. And all traces of the nursery were gone. Doris herself had seen to that.

She was relieved she'd remembered to push the old cabinet back in front of the tunnel door. Pike hadn't made it to the cellar yet, but Doris had no doubt that would be his next destination. She pulled again on the handcuffs. Pike had placed them around her right wrist and then attached the other end to the heavy fireplace andiron. Then she looked down at her thin wrist. If she turned just so…

From above she heard his footsteps once again. He was coming down the stairs. As he passed the library door on his way to the kitchen he looked in at her. "Where is she?" he demanded. Doris stuck her chin out stubbornly and looked the other way. Pike rushed off toward the kitchen. She listened for the sound of him opening the cellar door, then she turned back to the handcuffs. She twisted her body slightly and then pushed backward as far as she could to give herself the most room to maneuver. She clenched her fingers together, flattening and compressing her hand as much as she could and then slowly, methodically eased her bony hand out of the handcuffs.

Doris smiled to herself. She removed her shoes and walked softly and quickly over the soft, wool carpeting to her husband's large, mahogany desk. From the center drawer she removed a key and used it to open the bottom left drawer of the desk. There, lying in an open wooden case was the handgun Glenn had kept loaded in case of emergencies. She picked it up, liking the weight of it in her hand, remembering when she'd gone with Glenn to the gun range to learn to shoot. Just in case, he'd told her. She smiled remembering how the instructor had told her she had an excellent eye. She shoved the gun into the deep pocket of her cardigan and headed for the cellar.

55

At the top of the cellar stairs, Lucien flipped a switch and the lower level of the house was bathed in stark light. He took the stairs quickly, his practiced eye scanning the area, which was essentially open and contained the cast offs of several generations of Waldemars, dusty with disuse. "Nora!" he called, then listened for a reply. For anything. Quiet permeated the space. Upstairs the Waldemar woman had finally stopped her squawking. Maybe he shouldn't have handcuffed her the way he had, and he was pretty sure that move would earn him a write up from Captain DeBrun – or worse. Especially if he couldn't find Nora – or any proof of wrongdoing. He knew he should have called the station and waited for the uniforms to arrive before beginning the search but he hadn't wanted to waste any time. What if Bernie was right and Nora was in danger? What would he do if something happened to her?

He quickly searched every corner, looking for any sign of her. There was nothing. The cellar of the Waldemar estate was like a million other cellars, a place for discarded things. A workbench full of tools, a laundry room. The only two doors he found led to a small, empty wine cellar and a storage closet lined with shelves that had probably, at one time, been used to store canned goods. He stood in the center of the basement, turning again, trying to determine whether he'd missed anything. The next search would include the grounds, and he knew he would need to call in for help for that. The Waldemar estate covered several acres, which he knew he'd never be able to search alone.

He rubbed his hand over his eyes. Why hadn't he called her back? He'd never have let her come here alone. He put his hand in his pocket and wrapped his fingers around the cell phone he'd taken from Doris Waldemar. She'd also had Nora's Jeep keys. What could a woman as elderly as Doris possibly have done to her? She was tiny and had to be, in Lucien's estimation, well into her eighties. He liked to think that it was impossible that she could have hurt Nora. But Lucien had seen many different types of perpetrators hurt people in many different ways – ways you'd never expect - and thinking about that made his stomach clench.

As he turned, something caught his eye. Something bright, catching the overhead light. On the wall, completely out of place, near an old, wheeled law library shelf was a key hanging on a nail. What did it open? Lucien stood, looking for the door it might belong to – if it were the key to the wine cellar or storage room, wouldn't it have been hung near one of them? Then he saw it, in the dust on the floor – faint drag marks that looked as if they matched the wheeled legs on the library shelf.

He quickly dug in his pocket for his penlight and flicked it on, then shined the bright light along the base of the wall and could see that the shelf was hiding another door. "Nora!" he shouted. Hearing nothing, he shoved the shelf out of the way, revealing thick oak set into a cement frame. He fumbled with the key, pushing it into the lock and turned it hard, listening to the squeal of rusty metal.

Lucien pulled the door open. It flew against the cement wall with a thud. He shined his light down the tunnel, found the switch on the wall and flipped it, flooding the area with weak, yellow light. At the end he saw another door. There was a chair sitting in front of it. On the floor was an empty glass. He picked it up and sniffed. Scotch. He banged on the door. "Nora! Nora! Are you in there?" He pulled on the door to no avail, then turned and ran back down the tunnel, extracting the iron key from the first door, and returned to the end of the tunnel.

He placed the key in the lock, thankful that it fit, and turned it. As he hauled open the door, the first thing he saw was a column of misty light that seemed to retreat into a corner. Nora was lying on the floor in the center of the room. Leaning against the wall near the coal chute door was a decomposed body. Lucien winced, dropping to one knee and cradling Nora in his arms. At first she didn't stir, her face was ashen. There was a deep gash on her head, badly bandaged, and congealed blood on her face.

He brushed at her face. "Nora," he said softly. "Nora, please baby, open your eyes." There was nothing. She seemed to be barely breathing, and fear like ice settled in the pit of Lucien's stomach and along with it, anger, cold as steel.

And then her eyelids fluttered. She sucked in a breath, wincing with pain. She opened her eyes and looked up at him, confused. "Hey," he said, stroking her cheek softly. "There you are. It's okay, Nora. I'm going to get you some help."

"I don't think so," said the steely voice behind him. As Lucien turned his head, he heard the unmistakable sound of a gun being cocked. Once again he looked into Doris Waldemar's eyes – and the down barrel of a Smith & Wesson.

56

When Lucy touched Daddy's hand it was if all the stars in the sky exploded around them, turning pink and yellow and blue. She was filled suddenly with light, and for a moment could look across the pond and see it as it once was, beautiful and green and magical. Lily had stopped crying. In fact, she was uncharacteristically mute, with joy Lucy supposed. She thought about the last time she'd seen her father. It had been the night before he'd gone to Chicago. He'd come up to the nursery and sat on the floor between their beds, stroking their small heads with his big, warm hands. It was nice and had made

Lucy so sleepy. She remembered fighting it, wanting to enjoy her Daddy as long as she could. Mummy would be with them while he was gone, and with Gran gone, too, it was not a good prospect for Lucy and Lily.

It had been Daddy she'd missed the most, although she and her sister were also desperate for their Mummy – the Real Mummy, the one they knew and did not know. Now the pond was their Mummy, the great womb in which they floated waiting to be born. Real Mummy was Otherside, too, but they'd not been able to get to her, even though they knew she was near. She was trapped somewhere, just as she and Lily were trapped in the pond.

But now, here was Daddy, handsome as he ever was, holding his arms out to them. The girls rose together, hand in hand as they had been since conception, connected, one. Daddy took their hands, then unable to stop himself, wrapped both his daughters in his arms in a bear hug like he'd done so many times before.

"Let's go find your Mummy," he said, and Lucy and Lily knew he meant Real Mummy. That they would all be together at last.

"Yes, Daddy," they said at the very same time.

57

Doris held the gun steady. She was quite proud of that actually, after all she'd been through today. And the drinks she'd had. But really, wasn't enough enough? Pike was down on one knee like a pathetic suitor, holding the girl who, Doris had to admit, really did look worse for the wear. The slightest bit of panic niggled in her stomach. The girl disappearing was one thing – but the cop? Surely, someone knew he was here. Her face was stony as she made her way carefully down the tunnel, keeping the gun steady. She was going to have to lock them in, give herself some time to think.

"Pretty picture," Doris said. "Lovebirds. How sweet."

"Put the gun down," Pike said. "You don't want to do this, Missus Waldemar. So, before you do something you regret –"

Doris broke into peals of laughter. "Are you serious?" she asked Lucien.

The girl was pushing herself up. "She – killed Bettie," Nora said. "And the twins."

"Twins?" Lucien said. "What twins?"

"And Glenn. Her husband." Nora propped herself up against the wall, trembling.

In the tunnel, the lights flickered briefly. Doris looked up and Lucien took the opportunity to rise up and take a step toward her. Doris turned to him with a snarl, pointing the gun directly at his head.

"No!" screamed Nora. "Lucien! Stop!"

He raised his hands, palms outward. "Doris," he said. "Let's talk – " He took another step, and Doris put her finger on the trigger.

"Please, Lucien!" Nora begged. "Listen to her. She'll do it!"

"That's right, missy," Doris said. "I will. In fact, I think it may have just become completely necessary –"

Doris stopped mid-sentence, her eyes becoming wide and round, focused on something behind Lucien and Nora. In the tunnel, the lights began to flicker madly. Lucien and Nora turned their heads. Doris stepped back, her hands shaking. Behind them Bettie Pepper rose up, her black eyes focused intently on Doris.

Behind her was a rustling. It was a hollow sound that chilled Doris to the bone. She wanted to turn, but was afraid to, and disinclined to drop the pistol. A coldness filled the tunnel and a sound like paper blowing in the wind, or leaves.

Doooorrrrisssssssssss……..

Slowly, she turned. There behind her was Glenn and the little girls, floating toward her hands outstretched. Bettie approached, meeting them, and as the four specters came together, connecting in an embrace that surrounded Doris, she felt as if ice had pierced her heart. The gun clattered to the floor and she was sinking into the darkness.

<u>58</u>

Nora sat in the rocking chair, staring out at the stand of birches behind her apartment. Why was it always this way between them? They were like two porcupines, she thought, full of stickers that prickled at one another. She closed her eyes and laid her head back on the chair, thinking about that night. He'd come for her, had saved her. And after…after… he'd brought her here from the hospital where she'd declined to stay the night for observation. He'd refused to leave her side. He'd tucked her in her bed, covered her with her favorite quilt. He'd been so tender, so quiet. For the longest time, they'd just looked at one another....what if...what if...it was obvious to both of them that they'd each been afraid for the other. And when his lips had come down and brushed hers, it had been like going home. So familiar and good.

But after that night – things had been strained. What if...what if... He'd been sweet to accompany her to Bobbi's funeral and was attentive to Bernie, helpful, quiet. Doing whatever was needed. His attention had felt good...too good, Nora knew. Just like she knew her part in pushing him away. They seemed to push at one another. Always.

Nora's mind went back to that night – the coal cellar, Bettie's moldering body, the gun pointed at Lucien. The spirits of Glen and Bettie and their children, reunited – the column of white light that appeared as they finally found one another, rising through the ceiling, perhaps each floor of the house and finally releasing into the heavens. At least she liked to think that was what happened.

Nora shivered. It all could have turned out so differently. Doris Waldemar, regardless of her age, had been remanded to jail to await trial after she'd recovered. Vivian had returned home and was trying to make sense of all that had happened in her childhood home. She'd come to Bobbi's funeral as well, approaching Nora hesitantly. Apologizing for the many things that weren't her fault. She sat beside Nora, at Bobbi's graveside. In the distance they could see the other mourners milling near their cars, talking in low voices. Lucien in a sleek, black suit was standing near Bernie, his arm around her for support. Several people were talking with her.

"We used to be friends," Vivian said again, just like she had weeks before. To Nora it seemed like it had been much longer.

"Yes," she said. "We were."

Vivian reached over and touched Nora's hand lightly. "Maybe we could –"

Nora looked into Vivian's eyes. Her face, she knew, was a stone wall. Vivian looked down and removed her hand quickly. She stood. She started to walk away, then had turned back to Nora. "I'm having it filled in. The pond now that – now that they - ."

Nora turned away from her and looked at the three new gravesites next to Bobbi's open one. "That's good," was all she said.

Nora sighed. Outside, the white trees were stark and beautiful against the setting sun. She knew why she loved the birch trees so much. They always reminded her of Lucien. So tall and straight, like white knights standing at the edge of the wooded lot. She picked up the phone then and dialed his number, listened to it ring and then go to voice mail. She pressed the button angrily, ending the call, not leaving a message. They hadn't spoken in more than four weeks, since the night they'd...

Porcupines, she thought. Would they ever be able to lay their sharp quills down? Or would it be forever like this? She rose and shook out her dark hair. The snowy coil that was a reminder of the ghost twins, Nora's long lost cousins, still hung in a tangle near her face. After Bobbi died, Nora hadn't been able to bring herself to have it colored. She wanted to keep it as a reminder of both her great aunts and the small cousins who'd died so tragically and so young.

She walked into the bathroom and brushed her teeth, and then pulled on the oversized tee shirt she liked to sleep in. She looked into the mirror. The cut above her eyebrow was nearly healed though she was pretty sure it would leave a scar. Another reminder. She put her hand on the light switch and turned toward her bedroom.

In the wastebasket, the plastic cylinder caught her eye. She bit her lip as she stared down at it and the big blue + that had developed on it that morning when she'd taken the test. What if...what if...she thought.

Nora Pepper snapped off the bathroom light.